TARGET -

By Christopher Coville

To my Family: my wife, Irene, and Peter, Nicky and Theresa.

And to dedicated and courageous service men and women of all Nations.

Order this book online at www.trafford.com/07-1059
or email orders@trafford.com

Most Trafford titles are also available at major online book retailers.

© Copyright 2007 Christopher Coville.

All rights reserved. No part of this publication may be reproduced, stored in a retrieval system, or transmitted, in any form or by any means, electronic, mechanical, photocopying, recording, or otherwise, without the written prior permission of the author.

Note for Librarians: A cataloguing record for this book is available from Library and Archives Canada at www.collectionscanada.ca/amicus/index-e.html

ISBN: 978-1-4251-2969-9

We at Trafford believe that it is the responsibility of us all, as both individuals and corporations, to make choices that are environmentally and socially sound. You, in turn, are supporting this responsible conduct each time you purchase a Trafford book, or make use of our publishing services. To find out how you are helping, please visit www.trafford.com/responsiblepublishing.html

Our mission is to efficiently provide the world's finest, most comprehensive book publishing service, enabling every author to experience success. To find out how to publish your book, your way, and have it available worldwide, visit us online at www.trafford.com/10510

www.trafford.com

North America & international
toll-free: 1 888 232 4444 (USA & Canada)
phone: 250 383 6864 ♦ fax: 250 383 6804
email: info@trafford.com

The United Kingdom & Europe
phone: +44 (0)1865 722 113 ♦ local rate: 0845 230 9601
facsimile: +44 (0)1865 722 868 ♦ email: info.uk@trafford.com

10 9 8 7 6 5 4 3 2

CHAPTER 1

2ND MAY 1982

Lieutenant Alfredo Sanchar shivered. This made no sense; for God's sake, it was stifling in the enclosed area of the ship's bridge. Self-consciously, he scrutinised the faces of his fellow seamen, but they hadn't noticed his discomfort. No, it was not the cold, he reasoned. There was something else, something very sinister, gnawing away at his subconscious.

Outside, over the top of the mighty six inch gun barrels that were raised for action, the bow of the venerable Belgrano gently rose and fell into the dark waters of the South Atlantic. The sea: massive, ominous, but so very seductive. This was why he had joined the Navy. He had fallen in love with the sea the first time his father had taken his two boys out in a small wooden boat from the harbour at Buenos Aires. Old Alfredo had smiled at their unconcealed excitement, as the flimsy craft rolled and creaked its way to where they could catch a few small fish to please their mother. The man had felt guilty at naming his first son after himself, as no more than 10 minutes separated the births of the two boys. But he had long before decided that this would be so, as his father had before him. To his relief this small privilege had caused no rancour between the two boys. As they grew, they became ever closer. To some their closeness was disturbing, but to old Alfredo it was a comfort. He had suffered a difficult and lonely childhood, and he and his wife marvelled at the friendship of their sons. It had seemed only natural when both told him that they wanted to join the Navy. Of course, Mama had cried as mothers always do on such occasions. But Alfredo was proud; his boys would help liberate the Malvinas and bring glory to the family's name.

But now, on the Battleship Belgrano, the 18 year old boy turned sailor for his country felt fear of the sea for the first time in his life. The sea had been his passion, but she could be a treacherous mistress, especially this one. Yes, especially this one, which lapped the shores of his homeland, and enveloped the Malvinas Islands. This dark, saturnine beauty had charms that would seduce a man into drowsy contentment. But she could change with the faintest shift in the wind. From the south, from Antarctica's frozen wastes, the wind brought snow, but snow that could clog a man's boots in minutes; snow that could not be denied access, but that crept into every room and every cupboard in even a tightly sealed ship. From the balmy north, the wind brought gently floating clouds that clipped the tops off ships' funnels. From the west, from the homeland, came snarling fronts and depressions, but their anger was short-lived, and in between the air was crystal clear, sweet to the smell, and beloved by the farmers, sailors and kelpers, who joyously filled their lungs with its cool sharpness.

Alfredo Sanchar liked the Westerlies, but feared most the gentle winds from the east, for it was here that the night conjured up banks of thick fog. Sailors over the centuries had learned to be wary of these misty blankets, which covered sound and cheated a man's natural senses: But today the wind was from the west, and although the sea was gaining more energy with every hour, he should have felt at peace. And yet the sea was taunting Sanchar; the wind's gentle howl brought not comfort, but an icy fear. It was the fear that causes the hackles to rise on an animal's neck when it scents the predator, the same fear which grips the fox as it hears in the distance the sound of the huntsman's horn and the baying of the hounds. He was being stalked.

Sanchar came back to reality with a start. He flushed as he realised that lost in his thoughts, he had missed the words of his Captain. "I'm sorry, sir, I didn't quite catch that," stammered Sanchar awkwardly.

The other young officers turned away to hide their smiles. "Lieutenant Sanchar," repeated Commandant Bonzo patiently, "for heavens sake, get below and take a break. You look as though you could do with some sleep."

Sanchar nodded obediently. Young officers learned very early in their careers that it was unwise to argue with this man. Ignoring the suppressed sniggering, Sanchar swung himself through the heavy metal door which led down into the ship's dark interior. The Belgrano was old. She was very old. To his shame Alfredo worried about his ship, although he loved her dearly and protected her name with fierce pride ashore. At forty-three she was twenty-five years his senior and nearly as old as her balding Captain. But far worse, she was badly prepared for this mission, and it was no secret that Bonzo had been furious with the Admirals in Buenos Aires, who had sat by and accepted her shabby condition and shortage of vital war supplies. Years of neglect told on the face and in the physique of this grand, majestic old lady who, as the USS Phoenix, had survived the Japanese attack on Pearl Harbour. That was good; she was a survivor, but she was getting too slow and arthritic to be out in these cold waters with the British task force not far away. Thoughts of the British brought the feeling back to Sanchar. He stopped at an open observation hatch to breathe in the fresh, cool, afternoon air. The sun was sinking into the sea, and in the distance, rising in and out of the gentle swell, he could just make out one of the escorts, the Destroyer Hipolito Bouchard. The raised his spirits a little. With a smile, he thought of his friend Juan Lopez, who was on board the attentive escort, and with Bouchard and her sister ship, Piedra Buena, in close attendance on their mistress, Sanchar felt more comforted.

The canteen in the Belgrano was cramped, and at whatever time of day it stank of overcooked vegetables. The head steward, the massive Petty Officer Orgino, had long since abandoned any hope of providing a proper service in his chaotic surroundings. But he was determined that Captain and junior hand alike realised that this was his corner of the ship. He was a fearsome bully; not with his fists, but with a biting tongue backed up by an ominous physical presence. No-one faced up to Orgino and no-one ever complained. It was a satisfactory arrangement.

Sanchar nodded at Orgino as he entered and received a token stiffening of the shoulders in return. Easing past the burly head steward he collected a large mug of muddy black coffee and an over-thick sandwich. Alfredo was not an aloof man, but he disliked the company of conscripts when he was eating. To him, eating at sea held no pleasure, and he could not generate the pretence of conviviality in such squalid conditions. Seeking a quiet spot, he squeezed into a corner and rested his back against the cold metal that resonated unevenly with the labouring of the ship's tired engines. Everyone was tense, and there was unmistakeable fear in the faces around him. Like him, they were young, his shipmates. The news of the British bombing raids on Port Stanley Airfield had shaken many Argentineans, but these wide-eyed youngsters had received the news with complete disbelief. These boys were not real warriors, and although the liberation of Las Malvinas had been greeted by them with nationalistic euphoria, they had been shocked back to reality when the British Task Force had sailed the eight thousand miles down across the face of the earth into their waters.

Sanchar could not bring himself to hate the British. In fact, underneath he had a sneaking admiration for their absurd determination to recapture the Malvinas. But their bloody-mindedness and the rantings of their Boadicean Prime Minister would surely lead their fleet into disaster. How could any navy fight so far away from its shores? Still, he could not work up the aggression necessary to face up to a fight, even though the events of the past twenty four hours now suggested that battle at sea was imminent. Alfredo shuddered again. To his shame, he realised that a few of the sailors nearby had noticed. It was bad enough to show fear to fellow officers, but to do so to these young sailors would serve only to make them even more anxious. Feeling his pulse begin to race, Sanchar picked up his mug and plate and made for the door. Orgino watched him deposit his crockery and uneaten sandwich in the kitchen hatchery with approval. If only all officers were so considerate, he reflected sadly, his task would be much easier. But something was obviously worrying the young Lieutenant, and Orgino sighed. He sighed in the way that older men often do when they see younger men failing to live up to their expectations. Many years ago, when he was a junior seaman, his officers were careful to conceal their emotions before battle, and he admired them for it.

Sanchar looked at his watch as he stepped down into the long, dimly lit corridor that would take him down to his unwelcoming cabin. It was four o'clock. Down below, in the black waters, two steel sharks throbbed their way towards Belgrano's fat, juicy underbelly.

The first explosion threw him violently across the passage. His right arm buckled under him as he tried in vain to reduce the impact as his head struck against a metal strut with a sickening thud. Wincing at the pain, he steadied himself against the cold wall and waited for his vision to clear. The second explosion burst his eardrums and forced the breath from his chest. Barely had the pain registered when a blinding sheet of flame engulfed him as it raced past down the gangway in search of more oxygen. Sanchar was thrown heavily to the floor, gasping through scorched lips for air. His lungs felt as though they were on fire. There was no light, no sound, just gathering darkness as his tortured body slipped slowly into welcome oblivion.

A sudden rush of icy water forced him back to consciousness, as the weakened outer plating in the canteen collapsed. The stricken ship groaned and lurched to the left, throwing Sanchar against the seaward wall. He now felt no pain, but only the animal fear that grips all trapped creatures. Gagging on the oily sea water, he used every ounce of his remaining strength, and pulled himself awkwardly to a crouch. In total blindness, he groped for the ladder that he knew would take him up to the open deck above. After a few yards he stumbled across the rungs and, sobbing with relief, struggled to pull himself up towards the open hatch. Another violent shudder pulled him off his fragile perch, and after holding on with straining arms for a few seconds, he dropped back down into the inky void below. Sanchar lay moaning in the deepening water, broken and exhausted. Feebly, he clawed the air. He had to catch hold of the slimy ladder rails somewhere in the dark above. But before he could a rush of freezing, bubbling sea water swept over him. The General Belgrano, the great survivor of the Japanese attack on Pearl Harbour, had used up her last ounce of luck and was heading for her grave. Lieutenant Alfredo Sanchar, son of Alfredo and Juanita Sanchar and beloved brother of Jose, took one last breath as his world turned from crimson to black, but his lungs sucked in only the cold, salty water of the South Atlantic.

In the lounge of the Junior Officers' Mess at Punta Arenas, Sub-Lieutenant Jose Sanchar was overcome with sudden anxiety. Something terrible had happened to Alfredo; he knew the signs. His head reeling, Jose sat down heavily, breathing deeply. As the world rotated around him, the compass needle of Jose Sanchar's life settled onto a new heading: in a direction that would lead him down a long and bitter trail of revenge.

CHAPTER 2

1ST APRIL 2000

At fifty years of age, Alberto Duartes was at the comfortable stage of life where he knew most people in the neighbourhood, and had few enemies. He had cycled this same route for nearly forty years, and he savoured the experience of patrolling his territory.

As he turned left out of the small square which surrounded his house, he swished through the tiny brook that constantly trickled down the gutter towards the sea behind him. Buenos Aires is a wet city, but even in a dry spell the brook in the gutter continued to carry with it the flotsam and jetsam that told tales of life on the street up which Alberto cycled.

Alberto smiled and pedalled with more vigour. He was glad Rosita was outside her small fruit shop today. She normally was, but realising that Alberto was always watching her, she tried not to be too obvious. Rosita Maduro was just a year younger than Alberto, and their lives had criss-crossed since childhood. Rebuking his saucy grin and flirtatious greeting, she allowed a few seconds to pass before lifting her eyes to watch the burly man cycling away up the hill to the meat factory. She remembered the first time he had kissed her at school, the time a few years later when he had taken her virginity in a damp field outside town, and brushing back the dark curls that fell across her handsome face, she shrugged off the feelings of sadness and regret that their clandestine affair of many summers had ceased long ago.

It was just as well, she reflected. His wife was a jealous woman, and Rosita had found his embrace less enchanting as the time passed. She sighed. Perhaps if her own man had stayed with her she would not have needed a worthless layabout in her bed. She would certainly have had less trouble with Sabina, the only child of her ill-fated and short-lived marriage. It was not easy for Rosita to scold her wayward daughter, for she saw too much of her own love of life in the girl. Anyway, things seemed to have settled down for a while, and she felt comforted that Sabina's charms had ensnared such a worthy prize. Captains in the Argentinean Fleet Air Arm were not found on every street corner, and this Jose Sanchar was definitely something special. It was only short term, of course. Sabina had met him at the nightclub where she worked most nights, and their relationship had developed into a regular pattern of weekly meetings that ended in Sabina's bed.

The woman smiled to herself as she carefully arranged the tomatoes to conceal those that had seen better days. It made her feel good that upstairs in her daughter's bed lay a man with so much power and influence; and he was generous too. As Rosita smiled, she closed her ears to the muffled sounds that had started to rise above the clamour of the street, from the window above.

Captain Jose Sanchar was choking, and blinding flashes cut across his vision. Frantically, he clutched the heaving moist buttocks that thrashed around beneath his writhing loins. Sabina squeezed the back of his muscular thighs between her soft, brown calves, and bit deeply into his shoulder as she struggled in vain to hold back longer the orgasm that threatened to tear her body in two. Together they soared away from earth, way into the depths of space, into a sky of shooting stars and crimson galaxies, before peacefully sinking downwards to a gentle landing back on the quiet Earth. Sabina gasped as his whole weight relaxed onto her slender frame, and then felt a growing alarm as the slow deep sobs of her lover started to take over from the passion of moments before. The girl did not fully understand, but she knew well enough that after physical release of their lovemaking, there would follow in her man a deep and painful outpouring of grief that frightened her.

Jose Sanchar wept and shook his head from side to side as he tightened his grip on Sabina's shoulders. She winced with the pain, but hid her discomfort. Whatever his secret wound, Sabina knew that he had to release the tempest inside him. Had she but known what lay ahead, she would have rid herself for good of this haunted man. But how could anyone know that the Commanding Officer of Puerta Belgrano Naval Air Base was hatching a plot to wreak bloody vengeance on the British.

Captain Jose Sanchar dressed quickly and left Sabina sleeping in the cool of the morning. Rosita bid him farewell formally as she always did, but was quickly indoors to confirm that he had left her the money on the kitchen table. She smiled and tucked the notes carefully under her blouse. It was true that Sabina did all the work for this man's kindness, but had not Rosita had to do the same many times before when she had a baby to support by herself? She felt no guilt. As she walked outside the shop, she could make out Sanchar's car disappearing out of the square at the top of the street.

Sanchar yawned and shook his head to waken himself properly. He swore as a car cut in front of him at a set of traffic lights. A hand appeared from inside the mud-encrusted vehicle and poked a finger at him. But that was the end if it: tempers were lost but regained with as much speed in the traffic of Buenos Aires. As he drove out of the city onto the open road, his mind began to drift and go over the events that led to this crucial phase in his life. It seemed to him hardly possible that nearly eighteen years had passed since Alfredo had died in the war of the Malvinas. The body had never been found, and wherever the rusting hull of the Belgrano lay would forever be his brother's tomb. However hard he tried, Sanchar couldn't shake off the picture of his brother's lifeless eyes, his body slowly drifting backwards and forwards in the Atlantic current.

Jose had fought a bitter battle during the War, but it had been hopeless. The Mirage fighters that he had been flying, although capable aircraft and loved by their pilots, had had neither the range nor the firepower to go the distance required and then fight the British Harriers. His rage when the white flags flew over the Argentinean Garrison in the Malvinas had alarmed his friends and family. Broken by grief, his father had died within days of the defeat of his homeland, and his beloved mother lasted only a few months longer. Jose had not been able to console or comfort them, so stricken was he with his own grief and shame. And so he had been left alone, his family all gone in less than six cruel months; and it was the British who had changed the whole pattern of his life.

After the war, he had taken a month away from work and had sunk himself in physical exertion in the towering volcanic peaks of Patagonia. For a time, he thought it might be possible to put it all behind him and get on with his life. But Alfredo's lifeless eyes kept coming back to haunt his dreams. Slowly, in the solitude of that frozen wasteland, he had decided that whatever the personal cost and sacrifice, he had to avenge his brother's death.

When he had returned to duty, his colleagues had been bemused by his new single-mindedness. Few found they could or even wanted to compete with his ambition and dedication to work. He had lost what few friends he ever had in his increasing introspection, but this didn't bother him. When he had to display charm, for fear or for favour, he showed he could do so with the consummate ease that characterised his professional expertise. Gradually, he had passed by his peers in the Naval Air Arm and was now recognised by all as a rising star. Some thought that before long he would be the overall commander of naval aviation, but this was of no interest to Sanchar himself. For Sanchar had reached his major goal: he was the Commander of Number 3 Wing at Puerta Belgrano. He now had under his direct command a formidable force of fighters and fighter-bombers, but most importantly, he had control of the Squadron of aircraft that had nearly turned the tide of battle in the Falklands war - the Super Etendard armed with the missile whose name struck fear into the hearts of every sailor on the sea: Exocet.

CHAPTER 3

Commander Roberto Mantana eased the throttle forward on the Dassault Super Etendard, and felt the push in his back as the aircraft smoothly accelerated to four hundred and eighty knots. Out on his left, at a range of about two miles, he could see his wingman, Lieutenant Patricio, holding station accurately as the speed increased. Out in front, the two Mirage 3 escort fighters started to scan the sky ahead for any hint of the opposing fighters. Mantana checked his stopwatch. It confirmed the indications on his Singer-Kearfott navigational display that the target ship should be at about forty miles. Gently easing the nose of his aircraft up, he switched on the long range search radar. After flashing a couple of times, it settled down into a characteristic sweeping pattern. The target appeared as a bright blip on the speckled background of the cathode ray display.

"Contact zero nine zero degrees forty miles," Mantana transmitted, and rapidly dived down again to skim the white-topped waves.

Patricio excitedly waggled the wings of his aircraft in acknowledgement. Banking steeply away from each other, both aircraft eased out to form a pincer attack against the closing target, on this practice run a large floating platform moored several miles off the coast of

Argentina. Twenty miles; time to break radar cover and start the attack:

"Climbing,' called Mantana But they had been seen.... the two escorting Mirage fighters suddenly pulled up.

"Bandits! Bandits! Zero nine zero degrees, fifteen miles, coming towards," warned the lead fighter pilot, his voice betraying the thrill of the hunt as it neared its climax.

The enemy, being simulated by four other Mirages, pounced from high level, slashing down aggressively towards their quarry. The attack formation was in trouble and would have to get away fast to survive.

"Buster! Buster!" Mantana called over the radio, and both Super Etendards accelerated to maximum speed, leaving creamy wakes in the sea behind their screaming jetpipes.

Almost immediately, Mantana's radar warning system alarmed, alerting him to an immediate threat from a fighter's weapons system. In desperation he released a stream of chaff bundles from the dispenser under his wingtip, hoping that the tiny strips of metal would confuse the Mirage's radar picture. As he searched behind him, he briefly caught sight of one of the enemy fighters which had managed to disentangle itself from the aerial combat above. It was soon on to the fighter bombers. "Shackle," ordered Mantana, and both aircraft turned hard towards each other, threatening to sandwich the lone fighter.

He groaned as the massive forces of gravity dragged him down in the cockpit .... his vision dimmed .... he gasped for breath .... back off on the 'g' before it gets too much!

"Shit," swore Mantana, as the attacking Mirage pulled high.

Heavily armed, they could not match his climb rate, and he needed only to sit above and wait for them to turn back towards the target. They had to avoid the deadly attention of a Matra Magic infra-red seeking missile. Mantana seized the opportunity presented by the momentary respite, and dived back towards the waves at maximum speed .... his chest rose and fell in jerks .... the wet smell of the rubber oxygen mask was intense .... his throat was drier than the desert wind. They were almost at firing range. Feeling the hair on the back of his neck rise, he pulled up for the final phase of the attack.

"Firing, firing, now," he shouted over the radio, ensuring that his recording equipment was switched on.

In the subsequent debrief it would mark the point at which the deadly AM39 Exocets would have streaked from the underwing pylons at nearly 700 miles per hour towards the target. It was over.

"Stores away, knock-it-off," called Mantana over the radio.

Patricio pulled up and rolled his aircraft jubilantly. On this occasion they had completed their mission successfully; but it had been too close, he reflected grimly, as he wiped the beads of cold sweat from his forehead. Had he not told Headquarters time and time again that until they received the new electronic radar jamming device, they would be at the mercy of the fighters? Everyone kept nodding and agreeing with him, but as usual, it seemed to be taking an age for the trials equipment to arrive. Now if only he could talk to the Admiral himself sometime...

"Close echelon port," Mantana ordered and Patricio closed up for the final run into the airfield at Puerta Belgrano.

They cruised in over the cliff tops, ensuring that there was sufficient spirit in their arrival to let everyone on the base know that they were back. Touching down at 170 miles per hour, Mantana streamed the large brake parachute and gently brought the aircraft down to slow speed before taxying off the runway. The Super Etendard nodded forward as it came to a rapid halt on the wide aircraft parking area, and before closing down the engine Mantana cleared the groundcrew to insert both chocks in front of the warm mainwheel tyres. He smiled as the engine slowly wound down, enjoying the feeling of being physically and mentally exhausted after a successful and hard-fought combat mission.

He sometimes wondered why he stayed in the Armada, when more money and greater prospects were on offer elsewhere. But at moments such as this, when his heart pounded and his blood coursed through his veins, at times such as this, he knew the answer.

The six Mirage 3s involved in the exercise were already parked and he could see the pilots strolling together towards the hangar. As usual, attackers and defenders were arguing, hands floating around descriptively and voices raised in excitement.

Debriefing complex sorties was never easy, as memories faded with the passage of time. Fighter crews realised only too well the advantages of getting a bid in early, especially if the going was likely to get tough later on in the crewroom.

Mantana was rejoicing in the luxury of his shower when his bespectacled, worried-looking PA poked his head nervously around the bathroom door.

"Sorry to disturb you sir. It's the Base Commander. He wants to see you in his office - soon as possible."

Mantana cursed loudly. Petty Officer Costa quickly took the hint and dismissed himself to the sanctuary of his small office. He liked his boss, but he had never learned to repress the slight fear that military men often harbour for their seniors. It was irrational, because Commander Mantana was a considerate and sensitive officer, yet there was an unseen side to his character that frightened Costa. Perhaps it was the paradox of a quiet man climbing into an aeroplane and immediately becoming an aggressive demon. How could he do it? How could a man be one thing one minute and be so different a moment later? Costa shrugged his shoulders. These things were too complicated for a petty officer. With a sigh, he returned to his mountain of paper work.

Still feeling aggrieved at having to cut short his shower, Mantana entered the Captain's outer office. He nodded to the Base Senior Engineering Officer, Lieutenant Commander Aries. As expected he received a scowl in reply. There was no love lost between these two men. Aries had risen from the ranks, and was determined everyone should realise it. Over the difficult years as he worked his way up, he had developed a burning resentment towards the status and attitudes of the aircrew. He had hands etched with deep scars to show for his thirty years as an engineer, and he loathed the cavalier approach the pilots loved to display towards the aircraft that he and his men slaved to maintain.

"What's this is all about?" Mantana asked.

"I have no bloody idea," snorted Aries, "but I do know that it's keeping me away from my job." Mantana tried hard not to smile.

There was a noise from the office and both men stood up somewhat self-consciously as Sanchar opened the door. He nodded cheerfully towards them as he was finishing off some dictation with his secretary.

"Come in, gentlemen. Sorry for dragging you across

here at such short notice, but I've got some good news for a change." They looked sceptical.

'Really, it's good news. Come on in. You know where the coffee is."

Brightening, Aries and Mantana followed the Captain into the office and accepted his gesture to sit down. They sat patiently whilst he unbuckled a bulging file and extracted a long signal. It was Top Secret.

"The new radar jamming pod will arrive next week," Sanchar announced. This was indeed good news. Sanchar went on excitedly. "At first we shall get just two trial fits, and it will be left to us to test out the equipment on base. Then and only when we are perfectly satisfied with its performance, I have been authorised to make one Exocet firing, under full combat conditions. That'll mean as realistic a sortie as we can mount, with an opposing fighter."

"That's great news sir," exclaimed Mantana, "there are still a few old cynics around, but this should convince them that the missile will work properly with the pod operating at full strength. I guess we'll be planning for fighter escort and a Mirage attacking formation?"

Sanchar shook his head. "No, I did think about that, but I want the fighters to be sure of getting in behind the Etendard, to see if their radar can pick up the Exocet after launch. It's just possible that the pod will protect the mother aircraft, but that's no use if the fighters can still chase down the Exocet and destroy it with their own missiles."

"For the purposes of the trial, I'm happy that we just have one defensive Mirage to attack the Super Etendard. And obviously, there's no need for the fighter to be carrying live weapons. Let's try and keep it fairly simple."

"I take your point, sir, although we're bound to lose some element of realism. Talking about which, have we got a proper target this time?"

"I thought we'd use the old tug," replied Sanchar. "She's been lying in the harbour for six months now, and I can't think of a better way to put her finally to rest. Headquarters are happy with the idea, so now it's up to us to construct the right profile and get the trial going as soon as we can. That's where you come in, Carlos," he went on, turning his attention to the glum-looking engineer. "Start preparing two of our best aircraft now, with the emphasis on checking out the radars and navigational equipment. I want it clearly understood that I won't tolerate any delays with unserviceable aircraft during the trial. Now let's get going. Plan on finishing the initial pod trials by the end of next month, and if all is OK at that stage, we'll look towards the Exocet firing for the following week, during the late afternoon. We can fine tune dates and timings later."

"No problem, sir," said Mantana enthusiastically, "I'll get my weapons specialist working on the profiles today."

"I'm not sure about getting those radars checked out..." started Aries, but the Captain's sudden stare suggested he was not to be dissuaded. Both men saluted and left the office.

"Oh, one more thing, Roberto," called Sanchar, "I want to do that Exocet firing myself."

Mantana concealed his surprise well. "Of course sir," he acknowledged. "I'll arrange for a practice run for you over the next week."

As the door closed, he swore quietly to himself. Had the Captain not insisted otherwise, this could have been a golden opportunity for Mantana to achieve a rare live firing for himself. Still, the Captain was the boss.

Sanchar smiled as the door closed. He was lucky to have such good men working for him, he thought. Reaching for a cigar, he sat back and cast his eyes across

TARGET - THE QUEEN!   *Christopher Coville*

the map on the office wall. At the top of the chart lay the vast tropical rain forests of the Amazon; at the bottom the horn of Patagonia jutted out into the Antarctic Sea. The distances involved were great. But yes, it could be done. Risky .... very .... downright dangerous. But, yes it could be done. He smiled at the photograph of his brother on the wall, and drew deeply on his cigar.

CHAPTER 4

Richard Turnbull woke slowly. This was always the worst part of the day for him, especially after a late night. He had always been bad company first thing in the morning, and the slow realisation that he was facing another day alone didn't help much. Sleeping by himself in his double bed made him feel particularly lonely, and the unruffled pillow where Sally's head had lain until last week, heightened his feelings of self-pity. Turnbull grunted and shook his head to clear away the depression that struck him so severely first thing in the morning.

Yawning widely, he slowly straightened his back, stretched his arms up towards the ceiling, and after a few customary scratches made his way to the small kitchen. He liked his cup of tea in the morning. The process served not only to wake him up, but in the past it had given him the one opportunity during the day to do something kind for his wife. It obviously hadn't been enough.

Richard reached for the radio and sat sipping his tea, staring out over North London, with the gently intrusive music of Radio Three in the background. He liked Stanmore, despite its reputation for being the final resting place for retired Jewish businessmen, or as so often happened, for their widows. In the car park below the third floor flat, his ageing Ford looked a little out of place alongside the rows of 3-series BMWs, much favoured by grey-haired ladies. Shrugging off the slight feelings of inferiority, he poured a second cup of tea, and relished the extra strength of the brew that completed the transformation from sleep to wakefulness. That was the easy bit, but the 15 minutes of hectic exercises that he had inflicted on himself for the past ten years were not so easy these days. He realised he was making it easier on himself and the thirty press-ups had conveniently dropped to twenty. Yet he still made the effort, and that was not bad for his age. Hmm, he thought .... for his age. Pausing to check his waistline in the full-length bedroom mirror, he continued the morning ritual. He was determined not to become seedy, as he had seen so many of his older single friends become once they passed forty. It was worth the effort of getting up half an hour earlier to get a bit of a sweat up and take a cool shower. After dressing, Turnbull reluctantly forced down a bowl of stale muesli and two pieces of toast. He didn't like breakfast and neither did his delicate stomach, which always cried out for antacid tablets half way through his journey into town. Fastidiously, he tidied up, brushed his teeth, and after a quick check for open windows set out for the short walk to the Tube Station. Nodding to the vendor, he picked up a tabloid newspaper and jostled his way down through the crowds to the waiting train. As the tube pulled away, Turnbull made the usual pretence of reading the paper, stopping only to admire the occasional bright young woman who tripped onto the train at one of the grey, suburban stations punctuating the forty-five minute trip into the centre of the city. There was a time when he would have stood up for one of these women to have a seat, but he got fed up with the derisory looks of his fellow passengers and, like them, now pretended not to notice.

Getting out at Charing Cross, Turnbull forced his way up the left hand side of the escalator and made for the well-disguised and well-secured office block just off Trafalgar Square. There were only a few offices, or so it seemed, most of which sported a selection of prim-looking, middle-aged secretaries, who were occasionally visited by anxious looking men in three-piece pinstriped suits. But behind the sober facade, the two-door lift led into a much larger, darker set of corridors and offices that housed the military intelligence counter-espionage section of MI5. Using his electronic pass, Turnbull gained access to the secure area, under the watchful eye of a wall-mounted video camera. Checking his watch, he realised that he was late again and the Special Security Group were already assembling for the briefing. As he crept into the back of the room, he noticed the local CIA agent talking earnestly to the Director of the Department, Sir Michael Townsend. Richard's boss made it clear that he had noticed yet another late arrival. To his surprise there was also an old SAS friend of his in the room and another man wearing an MOD pass. He was a new face in the building, but he looked very military.

Even in his dozy Monday morning state, Turnbull realised that this was not just the usual Monday morning operations briefing. "Gentlemen, now that everyone is here," said Sir Michael somewhat pointedly, "perhaps we can get started. Do sit down please."

The Director waited for the shuffling to settle down before he continued. "Last night, I was advised by the Foreign Secretary that as part of the millennium celebrations, Her Majesty the Queen is to pay a good-will visit next month to Brazil and Uruguay. It seems that the close relations that have been built up in the area, particularly with the Brazilian Government since the Falklands conflict, have produced a climate that would benefit from a Royal Visit. I need hardly tell you that UK Limited already has a large stake in South America. Therefore, the Secretary of State for Trade and Industry, who will accompany Her Majesty, is very keen indeed that we make more ground in what is seen as an expanding and potentially profitable market. There is, of course, an element of risk to the Sovereign in the area, mainly from internal subversive elements within the host nations. Nor can we totally ignore Argentina, even though it's eighteen years since our little, er, misunderstanding. The expert view, with which I agree," he added in his pompous way, "indicates a low level of risk from the Government or the Armed Forces themselves. Carlos Menem appears to have cooled tempers over the Falklands during the past few years, but nevertheless there are still a few hotheads around who could cause embarrassment. Although the final details are yet to be resolved, the outline plan involves Her Majesty and entourage flying, via our staging facility in Western Africa, to Brasilia. After two days of formal activity, she will fly to Rio de Janeiro for a further two days before sailing in an improvised Royal Yacht, which is being upgraded and refurbished as I speak, to Montevideo in Uruguay. I need hardly say that the ship will be crewed entirely by Navy and Marine personnel. For old time's sake, we are calling the ship Britannia." He ignored the chuckles; many had predicted that the scrapping of the old Royal Yacht would be a decision that would come back to haunt the Labour Government. "The return trip will be entirely by air via Ascension Island."

He paused, looking a little annoyed. "Yes, Group Captain." All eyes turned to the MOD officer who had dared to raise his hand.

"I take it that Her Majesty will be flying in a RAF VC10?"

"That is correct," confirmed Townsend dryly, "and the aircraft will have to pre-position at Montevideo in good time for the return flight. Naturally, the same applies to Britannia, which will need to plan to be in Rio at least two days ahead of schedule to cover for possible delays in transit. You will want to make a note of some dates."

There was a pause whilst notebooks were opened. "The dates we have at the moment are 26th April, transit to Rio, 30th April leave Rio, arrive Montevideo 3rd May and leave for the return to UK on 5th May. I would stress, however, that these are very provisional at the moment."

"What's the point of the cruise down from Rio?" asked the CIA representative.

"Yes, I asked that myself," replied Sir Michael. "It would appear that the FCO believe that the new, albeit less well fitted-out Royal Yacht would provide a fitting base for the Queen's activities in Rio, and the spectacle of her departure from the harbour would seem to be too much to miss. Additionally, it's planned to sail the Yacht past several ports and harbours in Brazil, at pre-appointed times, to enhance the PR value of the trip."

"Isn't that a bit risky?" someone asked.

"Well that's not our business any more I'm afraid," responded Townsend, but he made no attempt to hide his misgivings. "The decision has been made and that's why we're here today. As usual, time is very short, and it's our job to make sure that the security aspects are tied up properly. The Defence Secretary has already agreed to the deployment of an anti-submarine frigate for close escort and a hunter killer submarine will be in the general area if needed. There will also be an SAS presence on board Britannia, but both the Brazilian and the Uruguayan Governments are adamant that they will provide all protection on their own land, as well as out to the 12 miles limit of territorial waters. They have made it quite clear that they don't want this to be seen as a show of British military strength in the area."

"What about the air side?," the Group Captain asked, clearly feeling a little left out in what appeared to be a Royal Navy show.

"Well, that's the biggest problem, I'm afraid", replied Townsend apologetically. "The FCO are insisting on at least a token air cover when Britannia is transmitting international waters between Rio and Montevideo. I fear this will involve fighters and Nimrods, the latter to keep a surface picture of all sea plots in the area, and to be on standby for search and rescue operations."

"Christ," uttered the Group Captain in dismay "that's going to need a hell of a lot of fighters, and they're going to require tanker support from our Tristars."

"Yes, I appreciate that Tony," agreed Sir Michael, "but on the bright side, both the Brazilians and Uruguayans have agreed that the Tankers and the Nimrods, together with any necessary support aircraft, may operate out of their airfields. They have refused, however, for obvious political reasons to accept the armed fighters. I suppose that means that they'll have to operate out of Ascension."

"Or the Falklands, of course," agreed the Group Captain. "I'll need to get my planning staff working on that right away, but off the top of my head I can tell you that it's going to tie up a lot of aircraft."

"Well we may all have our own thoughts about that," said Townsend condescendingly, "but I suggest we now get on with the detailed planning. You can all pick up the classified information pack from my office before leaving. Turnbull here will be my day-to-day co-ordinator, so don't hesitate to contact him if you have any problems at all. Thank you for your time, gentlemen," Sir Michael finished dismissively. He turned towards Turnbull. "Richard, would you and Superintendent

Stevens pop in and see me in ten minutes please."

Turnbull caught Mike Stevens' eye and smiled stoically. He had worked with Mike before and they both knew from bitter experience that the next month would mean some frantic activity for them both.

When everyone had left, Turnbull whistled slowly. "Nothing like giving everyone plenty of warning," he remarked.

"Thank Christ no civilian transport is involved," commented Stevens. "At least the screening of personnel should be fairly straight forward. I suppose we'd better go and see your boss."

Sir Michael Townsend's secretary was a haughty spinster, who believed anyone without a knighthood was below her interest level. As usual, she hardly acknowledged Stevens' and Turnbull's presence. "Good morning Miss Harper," Turnbull said slowly and deliberately. "Sir Michael is expecting us." He decided not to curtsey as he had in the past. She wasn't renowned for her keen sense of humour. Feigning surprise, Miss Harper wearily stood up and escorted them both into Townsend's office. Turnbull was always mildly amused at the way he was formally introduced into the Director's presence, especially as they had worked together for nearly twenty years now.

"Please sit down, gentlemen," invited Townsend, not bothering to raise his eyes from the file he was studying. Signing off an enclosure with a flourish, he looked up with exasperation on his face. "Bloody silly business this," he remarked, emphasising his point with a rap of his pen on the desk. "Anyway, it's going to be your job to screen anyone who's likely to be on, or close to the Royal Yacht. You're going to have to make sure that the usual thorough search is conducted of the vessel before she sails. As you can imagine, the Navy are a bit miffed about that, but both the Home Secretary and the Secretary of State for Defence have given us a clear hand. After that, it's up to the SAS and the Personal Protection Staff, although as I mentioned, security in Brazil and Uruguay will be the business of their own police forces. By the way, I've learned that in addition to providing the usual satellite intelligence, the CIA has agreed to do some undercover work for us in both countries. I don't particularly like having to ask them for too many favours, but they do have easier access in Latin America these days than we do," he admitted regretfully. "Right," he concluded, "you'd better get stuck in."

"Oh, Richard, just stay behind a minute," he added, apparently as an afterthought. Superintendent Stevens closed the door behind him.

Townsend's face softened, and a look of concern took over from his usual air of pomposity. "Richard, I was sorry to hear about the trouble with Sally," he said softly. "If there's anything I can do, please ask - as long as it's not a request for time off."

"Thanks, Michael," replied Richard, feeling a little lost for words. They had joined the Service together and Townsend had always been the one who was going to get on. He was ruthless and ambitious and apart from the occasional moment such as this, Richard had only seen the autocratic, uncaring and aloof side of his character. This brief show of sympathy, transitory as it was, moved Turnbull all the more for its unexpectedness. He nodded appreciatively and left.

Stevens was waiting in Richards's office and had already found the makings of two cups of coffee. "Sugar?" he asked.

"Just one, no milk thanks," replied Turnbull, sitting down wearily behind his desk. This was all a bit too much at the moment.

"You look knackered, mate," observed Stevens. "Is Sally going through a randy phase or something?" he sniggered.

"Hardly," Turnbull replied, "She left me last week."

Stevens grimaced in annoyance at himself. "Hell, I'm sorry, Richard. That was stupid of me."

Turnbull smiled. "Not to worry. Perhaps it's for the best. She never could come to terms with the hours, especially as she still thinks I just work as an administrative officer in the Civil Service."

They both chuckled, despite the seriousness of the situation. After an embarrassing silence, Stevens coughed and opened his file. "This new Royal Yacht's in harbour at Southampton at the moment, having some work done for the trip. Probably the ice-making machine has packed up. Apparently it was some rich Arab's gin palace. I haven't spoken to the Navy yet, but I should imagine they'll be sailing in about ten days. Are you OK to leave for Southampton tomorrow?"

Turnbull nodded. "Yes, I could do with going away for a while. That bloody apartment of mine is just starting to get me down."

"Are you sure you're going to be alright?" Stevens asked.

"Don't worry about me, you just make sure you do your bit properly" Richard replied sharply.

Stevens raised his hands apologetically. "OK, OK, I'm on my way", he said backing out of the office slowly.

Turnbull finished his coffee with a gulp, burning the back of his throat. Christ, this was a hell of a tall order. And to make matters worse it looked as though he was going to get the bad end of the deal, stuck back in

England while the others headed for the sun. "What an overkill," he thought out loud. Reaching for the phone, he dialled the number in the building for the travel office. 'Who the bloody hell is going to try anything as crazy as attacking the Queen?' he asked himself, shaking his head in disbelief.

CHAPTER 5

"Coffee, sir?" Sanchar woke with a start. Slowly he focused on the face that was peering intently at him. "Coffee, sir?" the patient stewardess repeated, her voice a little higher and a little more questioning. Jose licked his dry lips, breathed deeply through his nose, and with excruciating effort, smiled and nodded. It always astonished him that, as with nurses in hospitals, airline staffs were only content if they were feeding you or straightening up your clothes. Grunting a token word of thanks, he gazed out of the window that overlooked the massive starboard wing and engines of the American Airlines Boeing 747. Checking his watch, he noted that they would be landing at New York in just over thirty minutes.

He had been to the city many times before, but this was different, and he felt more than a little apprehensive at the prospect. It was a shot in the dark, but he had to try, otherwise the chances of completing his mission were virtually nil. He had been very lucky at first. The telegram from the British Foreign and Commonwealth Office to their Ambassador in Brazil had been intercepted and decoded by the Intelligence experts in Buenos Aires, and his masters had seen fit to send him an abridged copy. But he could dig no deeper without arousing their suspicions, and he needed more information on the route the so-called Britannia would be taking from Rio to Montevideo. Fuel margins would be tight, and he would only get one chance. If he failed it would be a betrayal of his brother's memory. Sanchar opened his wallet, and as he did so often, looked down at the photograph of Alfredo. Closing his moistening eyes, he went over the plot again.

The seatbelt sign chimed on and passengers slowly returned to their seats as the aircraft banked to port and started its gradual descent towards Kennedy International Airport. Below him the skyscraper-festooned peninsula of downtown Manhattan tumbled its overcrowded contents into the Atlantic. In the far distance he could just make out the thin crooked finger of Long Island pointing out to the East, towards the British Isles. As the aircraft straightened on final approach, the setting sun threw dark shadows between the towering white and pink clouds.

At this time of day, the wind that blew towards the Hudson River was abating, but the aircraft still rocked gently as it descended below the sun's rays. In the streets below, a host of lights from miniature cars and homes twinkled out from the gathering evening haze. Through the side window, Sanchar watched the bright red and white airfield approach indicators come into view, and as the pilot reduced power on the four mighty engines, the aircraft crossed the white painted threshold and touched down firmly on the dark tarmac.

He always detested the arrival procedures in a foreign country, but this time it was even worse. Despite himself he smiled at his weakness. It was absurd that in a jet at sea level, he could face the heavy defensive fire from a Type 42 British Destroyer, but could never look a customs man in the eye without feeling shifty. Shuffling up in the irritable queue, he tried in vain to filter off towards a pleasant, motherly figure. Instead, he found himself behind a quarrelsome group who held up the flow for nearly fifteen minutes. This was not a good omen. Sanchar moved up to the desk and presented his papers. The immigration officer slowly thumbed through his passport and stared him straight in the eye.

"Are you here on business or on vacation, Mr Sanchar?"

"On...er... vacation," he replied lightly, grinning mischievously in the way that one man does to another when there's perhaps a bit of fun on the agenda.

The officer's face broke out into a smile. "OK, have a nice stay sir, but you watch out for those downtown girls; they'll frisk you for every dollar you've got," he chuckled, slapping Sanchar's passport down in front of him. He was obviously glad to see the end of the queue in sight. Trying to conceal his relief, Sanchar strode confidently through the exit marked `Nothing to Declare', and walked briskly towards the taxicab park. Waiting until Sanchar was out of sight, the immigration official pulled the perspex hatch down in front of his desk, raised the `closed' sign, and reached for his phone.

Sanchar settled back into the leather seats of his Yellow Cab. This was his third trip to New York, but he still marvelled at it all. It was not just the vastness of the city; he was used to that. What had always fascinated him were the sheer variety of its people and the extravagant grandeur of its buildings. It was easy to be distracted by the stacks of litter, and all too often the signs of human flotsam lying around the streets. But somehow, through this, the dynamism and elegance of the great city shone through. Two pretty girls caught his eye as they accelerated to beat a red traffic light. To his satisfaction he noticed that the skirts were short again this year. .

Sanchar settled back and started to think about food. He was a man who liked to eat, and in particular he enjoyed seafood. Nowhere in the world had he found lobster to equal those from the cold waters of Maine that he had relished many times before in Nico's, his favourite restaurant off Times Square. Despite his hazardous career, he was by nature a cautious man, and if he found somewhere he liked, he tended to stick with it rather than risking disappointment in something new. Sometimes it bored his girlfriends, but it was his style, and if they didn't like it they simply moved on. For the same reason, he had booked into a hotel he had used a couple of times before. It was small and modest, but was well positioned on the outskirts of Manhattan. The staffs were always changing round in New York, so they probably wouldn't remember him, which was a good thing. On this trip, anonymity would suit him very well indeed. After a short journey, he settled his taxi bill, and earned a pleasant farewell from the Brooklyn driver for his usual good tip. He had learned long ago that it was considered a crime in New York to reward too little for service, whether good or bad.

The hotel looked exactly as he remembered it. Slightly smaller than the surrounding buildings, it seemed warm and welcoming. Inside, a small entrance led to a deep-carpeted and spacious entrance lobby. The leggy girl behind reception flashed an enormous smile as she greeted him in a shrill Southern accent. Creole, by the look of her, thought Sanchar, and quite attractive.

"Sanchar, I have a room booked for two nights."

"Checking the record for you sir." she said chirpily. "That's right sir, with a bathroom, at the back of the hotel. Could you sign in, please." Sanchar signed the register and completed the usual card questionnaire. He often thought it was only used to remind visitors of their alien status. "How will you be paying, sir?" she drawled.

"Credit card," he replied, sliding an American Express Card out of his wallet.

She deftly swiped the magnetic segment through the machine, asked him to sign the counterfoil, and returned the card with a sexy smile. "Room 202 sir, second floor, first on your left when you leave the elevator. Enjoy your stay in New York, sir."

Sanchar smiled his thanks, and within five minutes was running a much-needed bath. He hated long-distance travelling, but the joy of warm water outside and neat whisky inside almost made it worthwhile. He sighed appreciatively as he sank into the soapy water and took a deep draught on a long, cold Bourbon. It tasted very good indeed. His eyes closed and he drifted into a light sleep.

Downstairs in the lobby, Suzanne hummed merrily as she tidied up the reception desk area. She liked Mr Sanchar. He was very good looking and spoke with an attractive Latin American accent; that was more than enough to get her tingling with expectation. To her annoyance, the front door opened and she had to put her fantasies to one side. The sight of her visitors did little to revive her bubbly mood. "Hi, Sam." she called out, forcing a welcoming smile to her face.

The uniformed police officer nodded curtly. He was accompanied by a man in civilian clothes, but he made no attempt to introduce him to the inquisitive girl. "Usual check, Suzanne. Who have you got in tonight?"

Looking exasperated, she pulled out the guest register. "You came in this morning," she protested. "Why the hell are you bothering me again tonight? I've got a hotel to run you know."

Officer Blackman ignored her outburst and thumbed his way through the book, stopping for his companion to make notes at the last page. He nodded to show he was satisfied. "OK, let's go," he grunted.

"And quit riding me so hard," Suzanne shouted after them. Blackman ignored the remark. After they had left the hotel, both men walked across the road towards a large, grey sedan. In the front seat sat two tired-looking men in heavy white raincoats. Neither looked up as the policemen approached to speak through the open window. "He's staying for two days, and he's using his own name."

One of the men nodded and wound the window closed. Thoughtfully, he pulled out a long filter cigarette, offered one to his companion, and shook his head in disbelief. "What in shit's name is the Commander of Argentina's biggest Naval Air Station doing in New York, by himself, at this time of year?" he asked.

"Perhaps he's on holiday," his friend replied.

"Yeah, well I can think of better places than Manhattan in April. Why the hell doesn't he go somewhere sensible like California? I think we'll just keep an eye on him for a while. Let's split up now, and you get back to me at six tomorrow morning. Unless I tell you otherwise, reckon on meeting me back here. I'm hoping he'll be safely tucked up in his bed by then."

"OK, I'll just check in with Langley and then get my head down for a few hours."

Gerard B. King of the Central Intelligence Agency drew deeply on his cigarette, settled back into the seat and gazed thoughtfully across at the entrance to the hotel.

CHAPTER 6

It was after ten o'clock before Sanchar left the hotel. The April night air was cool, and he shivered as the sharp breeze penetrated the material of his lightweight suit. It was only a short walk from the hotel to Nico's restaurant, and he needed the fresh air to clear away the effects of jetlag. As Sanchar turned into the main street on the other side of the road, King sat up attentively and reached forward to the ignition.

Sanchar had spent the last hour profitably. Scanning the New York Times had yielded two likely points of contact with NORAID, the Irish Republican Army's supporting organisation in the United States. One was their New York headquarters, and the other a bar that was used as a meeting place for sympathizers. He decided he would try the bar first.

Unaware of the car creeping along at a discreet distance behind, he turned into the narrow street that he remembered well and which brought him to the unpretentious entrance to Nico's Restaurant. Inside, the bar area was quiet and Sanchar settled down, as people by themselves so often do, at the edge of the long bar. "Drink sir?"

"Martini, please," he replied to the young Italian waiter. He knew they made them very dry here, with nearly half a lemon and lots of ice. That's they way they drank it in

New York, and when he was there he liked it that way too. Settling back with a dish of green olives, he studied the bulky menu with pleasant expectation. Sanchar was not a gourmet, but he did enjoy simple food and good service. Experience had shown him that you could expect both in a good Italian restaurant. He also enjoyed the total anonymity and the lack of pressure. In his daily routine, he was constantly plagued by subordinates and superiors alike, and the constant battle to keep the Wing's aircraft flying kept him at work for more hours than was healthy at his age. If only he had married, he thought, but he had not met anyone he liked enough, and he now accepted, indeed enjoyed, the solitude of bachelorhood. He also recognised that his longing for vengeance, with the swings in mood that it had brought, would make him a difficult man to live with. A clearing of the throat from the headwaiter standing patiently trying to catch his attention broke into his thoughts.

"Good evening, signor. Are you ready to order yet?"

"Is the lobster fresh?"

"Of course, signor. It arrived this morning," replied the waiter, somewhat aggrieved that anyone should even ask such a question.

"Lobster then please, and could I have a bottle of Californian Chardonnay to go with it."

"Of course, signor."

Sanchar was not a great admirer of American wines. He found them a little too soft and fruity as well as being overpriced for their quality. However, he was in New York and a French Chablis with Maine lobster didn't sound right.

He had just drained his second Martini and was feeling pleasantly intoxicated, when the headwaiter unctuously summoned him to his place, conveniently situated by the street window. Of the twenty or so tables, only a few were empty. He smiled to himself; it was a good sign when a restaurant was full on a Monday evening. Down below him in the street, New Yorkers were doing what they do best - being busy. Between mouthfuls of crisp green salad, topped with Roquefort dressing, he watched every sort of shape of men and women bustling by. He had long ago decided that he liked Americans. Despite the plastic sincerity and over concentration on material possessions, he loved their infectious enthusiasm for life. He often wondered, however, whether he could take their lifestyle in anything but short bursts; perhaps being an occasional visitor was best.

The lobster was as delicious as he ever remembered, and despite his earlier reservations it was well complemented by the crisp white wine, drier than he recalled from previous visits. He nodded approvingly as the headwaiter passed by on patrol of his territory. He was just forking the last lump of juicy white flesh into his mouth when a sudden burst of joyous laughter caught his attention. On the other side of the room, a couple about his age were monitoring the opening of their second bottle of champagne. Clucking in a mock reproach, the wine waiter flamboyantly refilled their long crystal flutes. Happily, they clinked the brim of each other's glass, and as if alone, they raised the drink to their lips, never for one second averting their gaze from each other's eyes. Sanchar couldn't help watching as the man reached across and fondly caressed his lover's hand, speaking softly as he did so. His earlier thoughts returned. This young couple were so patently in love; they had the joy of each other and he had no more than a lonely meal and the hatred that burned constantly inside him. Such doubts had come to him many times during the past ten years, especially as he got older, but they were transitory and melted away as the vision of his dying brother came back to him.

Sanchar declined dessert, indicating with both hands on his belly that he was well satisfied and had to have a thought for his waistline. The waiter chided him for believing what so-called health experts advised, but realising he was defeated, invited Sanchar to take coffee in the bar. He made his way into the cosy lounge and ordered a very large brandy. He sipped slowly from the huge glass, and reflected that what it lacked in quality it more than made up for in quantity and strength. It was when he was waiting for the delicious burning sensation to complete its journey to his stomach, that he first heard her unforgettable laugh. He looked up in time to see her tossing her blond hair back and re-crossing her slender legs. She was sitting on a high stool and was clearly sharing a joke with the barman. Feeling his eyes on her, she coolly turned her head and stared him straight in the eyes. A flirtatious smile spread across her pretty face. Sanchar almost blushed as a tingling sensation spread through his body. He tried to smile back, but it must have come across as a grimace. Looking puzzled, she turned back to the barman, and they resumed their friendly banter. He took another swallow, finishing his brandy and indicated to the barman that he would like another. It seemed even larger than the last one. "Compliments of the lady at the bar, sir. She asked me to say that she's sorry if she frightened you."

Sanchar felt foolish, but this time when she looked round he managed to smile shyly, then stood up and gestured for her to join him. To his great relief, she only hesitated briefly, before picking up her drink and making her way across the room towards him.

She was like a cat, lithe and smooth in her movements. Hardly looking at him, she sat down in the chair on the other side of the table. "Thank you. My name is Jose Sanchar."

"Oh," she said, clearly impressed at his foreign accent and gentlemanly manners.

"Kate Jensen." She offered her hand, which he raised delicately to his lips. She was surrounded by a tantalising fragrance that he breathed in as she looked at him more closely. "Are you on holiday?"

"Yes, I'm afraid so," he admitted. "Is it that obvious?"

"Foreign businessmen don't eat alone," she replied wickedly. He looked puzzled. "They get fixed up with dates, honey. It's all part of the deal," she explained.

"Yes, I suppose it is." He relaxed, and felt good in her company. He was surprised she was by herself.

She read his thoughts. "I'm a hooker," she explained as though she was speaking to a child. She realized that he was confused. "A prostitute," she said slowly, stressing each syllable. He couldn't conceal his surprise, and must have looked hurt. "I'm sorry …. Jose?" she said questioningly. He nodded. "But, I'm a respectable hooker."

Sanchar nodded again. "You certainly look respectable."

They both laughed, and he ordered two more drinks. They chatted affably, neither asking too many questions, but perfectly content for the relationship to develop at its own pace and level. It was nearly one thirty when he next looked at his watch. He looked up at her soft, hazel eyes. "Why don't you come back to my place?" she asked in a very matter of fact way. "For a nightcap." She laughed again.

⁂

He was surprised at the luxury of her apartment. Perhaps he shouldn't have been, he thought. After all, it wasn't just the oldest profession in the world; it was also very lucrative for the select few. It certainly was for girls who looked like Kate Jensen.

"Nightcap?" she asked, easing the light stole from her tanned shoulders. Sanchar tried to decline, but his voice caught in his throat. She laughed kindly, and held up her arms towards him.

After they made love, he fell into a deep, exhausted sleep. Kate let him lie for a while. Moving carefully so as not to wake him, she drew a cigarette from her bedside drawer, and lay back staring at the ceiling. She felt troubled. He had made love with a passion and abandon that frightened her, but when he sank back into her arms he had wept like a man in terrible grief. And he said some very strange and frightening things which made no sense. But now he was at peace and she softly stroked his still moist forehead. After nearly an hour of dozing and watching him sleeping, she shook him gently. "Jose. Come on lover boy, time to move."

He stirred slowly, blinked at her incredulously for a moment, and after realising where he was, slid swiftly out of the bed. Feeling a little embarrassed by her intent and unashamed appraisal of his physique, he dressed quickly and self-consciously, coughing nervously from time to time. He reached for his wallet. "Not necessary, lover boy. Just buy me dinner tomorrow night." Sanchar hesitated for a moment. It wasn't wise to commit himself. However, he reasoned, he should have finished his business by then. If not, well she was only a hooker. And yet ...

"I'll pick you up here at nine then," he offered.

"OK", she said mischievously, "Have a nice day." She laughed and despite himself, he smiled with her. "That's better. You look good when you smile. You want to try doing it more often, honey. See you tomorrow."

"Ciao." Sanchar saw himself out. In the lobby downstairs the concierge studiously ignored him, as concierges should. Pulling his collar up half in guilt and half to guard against the cool breeze, he walked out into the quiet main road and turned towards his hotel. It was a walk of a mile or so, but he needed the fresh air. Alone but for his shadow, he strode out under the starlit sky. He was tired, but he felt wonderfully alive. As he disappeared into the distance, a car door gently opened and two men briskly walked across to the entrance to Kate Jensen's apartment block.

CHAPTER 7

THE Lieutenant Commander nodded stiffly as Turnbull introduced himself and Superintendent Stevens. Turnbull was used to this sort of reception from military officers, most of whom took it as a personal insult that anyone felt it necessary to check up on them. This was especially true of security matters.

Turnbull cleared his throat. "Do you think we could find somewhere to talk quietly?" he asked, breaking the strained silence.

"We could go to my office," the officer replied dryly.

Turnbull smiled to himself and winked at Stevens. As expected they were not going to have an easy time with this one. Grudgingly, Lieutenant Commander Hemsby RN led them past the Ministry of Defence Police picket post, and settled them down in his barely furnished, dingy office. "Coffee?" he asked. They both nodded. Turnbull reflected on the fortunes of a man who had obviously seen military action, judging by the row of campaign decorations on his chest. In the twilight of his career, he had been put out to grass. Turnbull wondered if this was how he would end up when the system had squeezed every last drop of blood from his body.

"Frankly, I don't know what the hell you're doing here," Hemsby said, slopping coffee as he thumped the two cups down on his desk. "Help yourself to sugar." They declined and winced as the powdered milk, which Hemsby spooned out, coagulated on the top of the coffee.

Turnbull spoke first. "We've been detailed to review the security procedures in dock before the so-called Royal Yacht sails for South America. After that it's up to you and the, er, additional gentlemen," he explained making some allowance for the need to keep the SAS presence on a 'need to know' basis.

"You don't need to worry," Hemsby replied sarcastically, "I may be kept in the bloody dark but I do get told some details." He was enjoying being on home ground, and was clearly relishing the process of making his guests feel ill at ease. "Anyway, who's put you up to this?"

Stevens reached into his pocket and drew out a very formal looking envelope, embossed in green. Hemsby leaned across and scanned the smart typescript. "Christ," he exclaimed, "It's from the First Sea Lord." "Quite" said Turnbull, realising that it was time to turn the tables. "And you had better change your bloody attitude right now if you want to keep your pension. Understand?"

Hemsby nodded. He didn't have much choice.

"Good. Now let's start with some sort of map of the dock area."

Stiffly, Hemsby unlocked a cabinet and without speaking unrolled and spread out a large white chart. It took a while for Stevens and Turnbull to orientate themselves, but it was obvious that covering the vast perimeter area was going to be a headache.

"How is the perimeter fence protected?" asked Stevens, obviously sharing Turnbull's concern.

Hemsby ran his hand around the chart. "We have a permanent guard on foot and by night we use dog patrols. In addition, all entry points have at least two men and are covered by close circuit television. No one, and no vehicles, are allowed in the area unless a current security pass is shown."

"And who issues the passes?"

"I do," replied Hemsby, "and I only do so after one of my men has thoroughly checked and verified the details on the application form." "What about the civilian contractors who are doing the refit?" Stevens enquired.

"Well that is a bit more difficult," Hemsby confessed. "They do tend to change people a bit more often than I'd like, but the firm themselves vouch for each worker. And they are never under any circumstances allowed anywhere near the Yacht unless a naval policeman is in attendance. I can assure you that this rule is never broken."

Turnbull nodded approvingly. "How much longer will the contractors be working on the boat?"

"Ship, if you don't mind," Hemsby corrected acidly. "They have been told to finish work by this Friday, which will give the weekend for a thorough search before she sails on Monday."

Satisfied with the geography, Turnbull left the map and returned to his lukewarm coffee. "How many people have you got on the sweep party over the weekend?"

"Including civilian police, nearly fifty. That's normal and all involved are experienced in the job. We also have four sniffer dog teams and two frogmen to cover the hull underwater."

Stevens decided to placate the aged sailor. "You've done this job before. Are you happy with the arrangements for security?"

Hemsby was caught off guard, but he warmed visibly. "Well it's always nice to have more people, but frankly a new man is a bit of a pain," he offered. "No, I'm happy."

"Well that's good enough for us," conceded Turnbull. "Would you mind if we just check through the list of contractors?" Chuckling, he added, "We've got to do something to earn our keep for the next week."

Hemsby now felt much better. He was getting proper recognition. "OK by me. I'll get my people to sort out a desk in the registry and have the cardex system put at your disposal. If I can help in any way ..."

Turnbull thanked him. They set to the tedious task of checking security permit issues against known agents. It was a boring job, but thirty years of experience told Turnbull that every now and again it was such a search which gave the vital clue. This time, however, it didn't and six hours later they sheepishly popped their heads into Hemsby's office. "We're off now. Perhaps you could let the Petty Officer show us around the dock area before we go."

"Go ahead," replied Hemsby. "I told you the passes were all in order."

He readjusted his reading glasses, sighed wearily, and got back to his paperwork. Stevens and Turnbull found their way outside and clambered into the back of the dark blue Land Rover. It was raining lightly and the cobblestones leading down to the waterfront were shiny and slippery. This didn't seem to concern their young driver, who tore off with both wheels spinning. They had obviously upset his boss, and he was going to show these bureaucrats from London a thing or two.

The docks were dirty, dank and inhospitable, and the awesome Yacht looked completely out of place. There were still a few people buzzing around on deck, but she was obviously nearly ready to sail.

Turnbull whistled. "She looks beautiful, doesn't she?"

"She certainly does. They've finished the outside. Just the work on the fittings in the Royal Quarters and some engine work left," explained the Petty Officer on guard, clearly claiming a measure of credit for the work done.

And so he should, though Stevens, remembering some of his early days as a bobby on the beat. He thought back to the many long shifts he had spent on diplomatic duties, protecting visiting statesmen. They never seemed to even notice him.

"I'd say you had this wrapped up very well, Petty Officer," he remarked. "Thank you, sir," the policeman replied gratefully. "It's not often we get anything nice said about us."

Stevens nodded in agreement. "Only the blame if something goes wrong, eh?"

"Nothing could go wrong sir. That's our job, isn't it?"

Two hours later, back at their small hotel, Stevens and Turnbull sat in a quiet corner of the bar. They were on their third whiskies, and were both feeling a little dejected. Stevens took a large gulp, and thoughtfully slid his glass around in a slow circular motion on the table. "You know, Mike, I think Hemsby's right. We're just a bloody nuisance here, and they've got enough to do already making sure this Yacht's cleared to sail by Monday."

Stevens shrugged his shoulders. "You may be right, but Townsend's obviously twitched up about this. He must be worried about his life Peerage."

"I couldn't give a shit about Townsend's prospects," replied Turnbull bitterly. "Christ, I wish all I had to worry about was when I was going to take my seat in the House of Lords." He drained his glass and banged it down on the table.

"Want to talk about it?" Stevens asked kindly.

"No," Turnbull replied curtly. "I'm sorry, Mike, but I need to be busy or I get too morose. What the hell are we going to do tomorrow ... and the next day?"

"I suggest we get on board the Yacht and do a bit of sniffing around. It won't do any harm for the contractors to notice us. Don't worry; there'll be enough to keep you busy. For a start we can sort out the layout of the ship in good time for the sweep over the weekend."

"That's true," agreed Turnbull, "But I've a funny feeling we're not going to be welcome there either."

Stevens sat back and thought for a minute. "If anyone is going to plant a bomb, it's going to have to be a big bugger to cause any appreciable damage. Right?" Turnbull nodded. "And there's no way they could do that without using at least one hundred pounds of plastic explosive. With nearly fifty people and the sniffer dogs, there's no way they could find a place to hide it away. What's more, you can bet your last fiver the SAS will spend the next two weeks in transit going over that boat, I mean ship, with a fine tooth comb."

Turnbull nodded slowly again. "You're right, Mike, so what the bloody hell are we worried about? Let's have another drink."

∽

Three thousand miles away in New York, Gerry King sucked his toothpick as he strode up and down the office. "For Christ's sake, Gerry, you're going to wear a hole in that goddamned carpet," drawled his companion.

King turned on him viciously. "It stinks, Pete. If this guy's as good in bed as Kate says, why the hell does he have to come to New York just to get a bit of tail?"

"Hey, come on Gerry, this really is getting to you. So the guy wants to get away from the office for a while and get stuck in to some pretty broad. What would you do? Don't tell me you'd shit on your own doorstep. Come on, pal."

King scowled. "Yeah, wise guy, but you don't fly three thousand miles for a sniff. What's wrong with Rio?"

"Aids", suggested Dillinger helpfully.

King ignored the remark and bit the end off a cigar. "I think I'd better give Dick Turnbull a call. The limeys have got this big push by the Queen in a few weeks. I know they think there's an Irishman with a Kalashnikov behind every tree, but when I was in London last week they seemed a bit twitched up about this one."

"But Gerry, there's no way the IRA could handle this, and the Brits and Argies have virtually kissed and made up," protested Dillinger. "Surely you don't believe they would risk trouble over the first visit by the Queen to South America in years? They wouldn't make any friends in Brazil or Uruguay if they did."

"Yeah, well you may be right, Pete, but I'll get on to MI5 anyway. And you can get off your butt and get our guys in Buenos Aires to run a full check on Sanchar. I want to know everything about that man, and I don't just want the usual crap they get from the military records. Tell them to do some footwork and dig deep for a change."

He looked at his watch as Dillinger reluctantly got to his feet. "When you've spoken to Argentina, Pete, get your head down. We're going to need some sleep before we latch on to Sanchar again tonight."

Dillinger wandered down the corridor towards the secure communications area. Carefully, he fed his plastic ID card into the electronic security system. After a few seconds a green light flashed and the large metal door eased open. He collected his card at the other side, and after checking in with a uniformed guard, entered a plastic shrouded phone booth. In minutes he was talking to the embassy in Buenos Aires. Judging from the attitude of the telephone operator, he had picked a bad time. Frostily, she asked him to hold whilst she located Second Secretary Ralph Prentice. It seemed an age before the phone clicked.

"Prentice here."

"Hi, Ralph, it's Pete Dillinger. Let's go secure now." Simultaneously they pressed the button on the receiver marked `Sec', and after a few flashes an amber light glowed steadily to indicate the scrambler was operating.

Dillinger moderated his voice to reduce the distorting effect of the system. "Ralph, it's probably nothing, but you probably know the Brits have asked us to keep our eyes open before the Royals make their visit to South America? Yeah. well, yesterday some Argentinean big shot called Sanchar pitched up at Kennedy. And surprise, surprise, our records show him as the big chief of Number 3 Wing at Puerta Belgrano. As far as I can see, the guy is just here for a good time, but the Boss is all twitched up. OK so far?"

Prentice's voice crackled back. "Yeah, fine Pete, keep talking. I'm just getting his details up on the computer."

Dillinger waited for the echo to fade away. "Well we fixed him up with Kate Jensen last night, compliments of the US government, and as far as she could tell he's on the level. The only strange thing she picked up about the guy is some hang up he's got about someone called Alfredo. Ralph, did you copy?"

There was a short period of silence before Prentice replied. He sounded excited. "Pete, you'd better listen to this. Sanchar is known to be a bit of a loner who keeps his opinions to himself, but from what we do know, he hates the British, and he's not afraid who knows it. And Pete, it seems he's got good reason. His twin brother's name was Alfredo, and he got the chop when the Brits sank the Belgrano. That was eighteen years ago this April and guess how old he was?" Dillinger's heart missed a beat. "Eighteen," he breathed.

CHAPTER 8

⌒⌒

Clancy shook his head. He reflected sadly on the care that went into the making of Guinness stout, of the trouble he took personally to ensure that bottles were stored at the right temperature and were properly rotated so that none went flat. He thought back to his boyhood in Dublin when, as the sun was creeping over the horizon, he would stretch his young limbs, yawn to the brightening skies, and watch the Guinness barges winding their way up the River Liffey towards the brewery and bottling factory not one mile from his home. Guinness was the pride of Ireland, and although Clancy's Bar had brought him a good living in the New World, he still despaired of the disregard these young clients had for the favourite drink of his homeland. He looked forward to nightfall, when his old friends gathered around, singing songs of Ireland, or martyrs and patriots and hunger strikes. But during the day the city slickers and tourists dropped in just to say they'd been there. Ah well, he thought, at least they pay the rent. He shrugged his malaise off as a foreigner asked for a refill.

Clancy raised his eyebrows. "You like your Guinness then do you, sir?" he asked with surprise.

"It's a new taste for me," replied Sanchar, "but I do find it quite pleasant" he lowered his voice, "I'm not a great enthusiast of American beer," he confided.

"Ah, you're right there, sir," agreed Clancy, "and you'll find Guinness improves with acquaintance."

They both laughed and Sanchar made himself comfortable on a bar stool. "Will you join me for a drink?" he asked Clancy.

"Well I don't usually drink before six o'clock, sir, but seein' as you're offering, I'll take a glass myself."

Sanchar turned his head in the direction of a sudden burst of laughter. Four youngsters were obviously the worse for the contents of several jugs littering the table.

"Black Velvet," explained Clancy with disgust. "Guinness and Californian Champagne. It's a sacrilege, but I make five dollars a jug on the champagne. Cheers and God bless you, sir."

They clinked glasses. Sanchar looked up at the impressive range of liquors. "What's that Irish Whiskey like? I've only tasted the Scotch type before."

"In the name of the Holy Mother, sir, you've been brought up very badly." Clancy reached up for a bottle of Jameson and poured two generous glasses.

"Salud," Sanchar toasted, and smiled appreciatively as the warm glow descended down his chest.

"Mexican, sir?" queried Clancy.

"Argentinean, but you got the language right Mr. er..."

"Clancy's me name," he exclaimed jovially, extending his hand in the sort of friendship that can only be spawned in such convivial surroundings. Excusing himself, he ambled to the other side of the bar to serve the noisy quartet. He looked very glassy-eyed, but still managed to open the eight bottles of Guinness with great style. Steadying himself he reached down and pulled two more magnums of champagne from the big old fridge.

Sanchar looked around him. It was a pleasantly scruffy place, bereft of wallpaper or carpets, but heavily adorned with Irish memorabilia. There were scores of photographs, paintings and slogans, most of them exhorting the British to quit Northern Ireland. Over in one corner of the bar was a large photo showing Clancy receiving a cheque from a dozen or so City types, and above it was a slogan seeking support for NORAID.

Clancy rejoined him. "Have another whiskey, Mr Clancy?"

"Just Clancy, not mister. No-one ever calls me Mister Clancy here. Yes, I'll join you for one more." They finished their drink as Clancy filled the peanut bowls. After getting a nod from Sanchar, he replenished their glasses.

"You on holiday, sir?"

"No, I came to see you, Clancy"

The Irishman looked startled. "Me!" He followed Jose's gaze up to the NORAID photograph.

"Clancy, I haven't got the time to explain everything." He moved forward and lowered his voice below the banter and bustle of the bar. His words had an immediate effect.

Clancy jumped as if he had been scalded. "Jesus, Mary and Joseph. Who the hell are you?"

Keeping his voice low, Sanchar told him only what he felt he must. It was sufficient for Clancy to know that he had a grudge against the British. The Irishman looked around him and nodded. "Give me your passport and get out."

Sanchar hesitated, but realised Clancy was holding all the cards. He quickly scribbled the address of his hotel on a beer mat and handed his passport around the side of the bar. As he left, Clancy returned to look after his noisy customers. He looked very pale.

∞

Sanchar had dozed on and off for about two hours when the phone rang. He jumped, sat up on the edge of the bed and waited a few seconds for his head to clear before lifting the receiver.

"Room 203"

"Mr Sanchar?" The voice was American.

"Yes. Who is this?"

"Just stay where you are for an hour, Mr Sanchar, and at precisely four thirty, go for a walk into Times Square. Don't look around, and don't talk to anyone."

"How will I know...?"

The phone clicked dead before he could finish. He put the receiver down, lifted it again and ordered coffee from Room Service. He was running the shower when it arrived, carried by a grinning young black steward in a sharply contrasting white jacket.

Sanchar tipped him a dollar, and grunted in reply to the hope that he should have a nice day. He drank the coffee black. It was good, but not quite as strong as he liked, and certainly not strong enough to clear his head after the whiskies at lunchtime. Still, in abundance it would produce the desired effect.

He stripped off, poured a second cup and took it through to the shower, which he had left running cold. Taking a deep breath he dashed under the fine, freezing spray, and roared like a bull as the shock sucked the breath out of his lungs. After suffering for nearly ten minutes he towelled himself down vigorously, and felt much refreshed and fully alert.

Outside, the sun was disappearing behind the Manhattan skyscrapers, and a light breeze was picking up the abundant litter that seemed forever strewn around New York's streets. It took him ten minutes to reach Times Square, where he tried desperately to look like an interested tourist. After twenty minutes, he decided to take a coffee in a small roadside cafe nearby. Despite two refills, there was still no sign of any attempt to contact him. Realising that he was wasting his time, he paid his bill ungraciously and walked briskly back to his hotel.

He had barely closed the door when the phone rang. Urgently, he picked it up and before he could speak, the same voice as before spoke quickly. "Go out of the back door of your hotel and wait in the alleyway. You are being followed."

The phone went dead. Sanchar swore. He was furious at himself for not having been more vigilant, but how had anyone got onto him? And who was it? Carefully, he opened the room door, and after finding the badly marked fire exit, descended down the two flights of the outside staircase to the rear yard. A dog barked from somewhere, but otherwise there was no-one about. Scarcely had he walked through the back entrance when a dark saloon pulled out of the shadows, and rough hands bundled him into the back seat. He knew well enough to say nothing and to keep his head down. After what he estimated to be about fifteen minutes, the car slowed and then stopped with a jerk.

"You can come up now Mr Sanchar."

It was the same voice he had heard earlier on the telephone, but in the darkness he could not make out any of the speaker's features. "Well, I hear you want to talk to one of our friends?"

"Yes, I need to see someone quickly, but he must be someone in authority."

"Mr Sanchar" whispered the voice impatiently. "You are not in a position to dictate terms to us. Now... Clancy has given us your story. Are you absolutely mad, or are you some sort of British informant?" The threat was barely concealed.

"I am neither. You've just got to trust me. I need your help, but in return I believe I can serve your cause."

"We don't like hare-brained schemes, Mr Sanchar. Exactly what do you have in mind to disrupt the Queen's visit to South America?"

"I repeat that I am only prepared to discuss this with someone in authority."

One of the heavily set men in the front of the car muttered threateningly, but the man with the familiar voice put a hand on his shoulder and silenced him.

They huddled together, talking quietly. The one in charge briefly jotted down a few words on a note pad, stopped and thought for a while and then tore the page out. He pushed it into Sanchar's hand. "Now go back to your hotel and take the rear entrance again. You are being watched by the CIA. They're in a white Pontiac, so make sure you're careful when you leave tomorrow morning. Here's your passport. Goodbye, Mr Sanchar."

Sanchar was pushed firmly out of the saloon onto the muddy pavement. After getting his bearings, he was surprised to find that he was only a few hundred yards from his hotel. He remembered the recent words of caution, but curiosity got the better of him, and trying to look casual he strolled down the side street towards the front of the hotel. It took him a few seconds to recognise the car, but when he did he felt annoyed at himself. He would need to be a lot more careful in the future.

Back in his room he dug out the crumpled piece of paper. Good...very good. A few telephone calls confirmed the necessary bookings for the following day. It always surprised Sanchar that his credit cards produced such rapid results in America. Back home, ordering aeroplane flights was usually a long and frustrating business. He was concerned about using his own name, but to do otherwise seemed pointless as his passport would be checked against his reservation. The duty receptionist accepted the early check out without fuss, and said she was sorry that he had been called back to Argentina unexpectedly. Sanchar smiled as he put the telephone down.

The impatient taxi driver grunted in relief as Kate trotted out her apartment block. Sanchar's heart missed a beat as he took in her sensuality. Even the driver's expression lifted as he looked her up and down.

"Hi, Jose," she greeted him, kissing his cheek softly as she brushed past.

She smelled marvellous. "Same place?" she queried.

"No, I've booked a table at a place on the waterfront. I hope you like Chinese?" Sanchar thought she looked concerned for a fleeting moment, but she brightened up quickly and touched his hand.

"You absolute rogue, Jose. How did you know I just love Chinese food?" They laughed as the taxi sped off and she moved up close to him. With so much on his mind he felt confused and had to keep reminding himself what she was.

She must have noticed that he was on edge. "You seem twitchy tonight, honey. Don't worry, Mama won't find out that her only boy is mixing with bad American girls."

He let the remark pass and it was soon forgotten as they arrived at the restaurant. Very soon a crisply dressed waiter was leading them to a table overlooking the Hudson River. Against his better judgement, Jose ordered the special banquet for two, to be washed down by champagne - French this time. Shrugging off her limp protest at such blatant self-indulgence, he poured the wine and they drank to each other, to America and to Argentina. She leaned across and kissed his lips gently, then excused herself pointing self-consciously to the

'Ladies' sign.

By the time Kate returned, two grinning Cantonese girls were busily laying out the crispy Peking duck. Jose got the feeling she was forcing her smile as she sat down, and he was surprised to see a slight tremble in her hands as she raised her glass to her lips. She finished her drink in one gulp, and noticing his concern, she wiped her forehead symbolically. "It's been one of those days. Any more of that delicious champagne, honey?"

"I've just ordered another bottle," he replied, and re-filled her glass.

"I think I'm falling in love with you, Jose," she said suddenly. He was stunned, and she must have seen it in his face. She held up both hands. "Hey…forget I said that. Let's eat - this looks fantastic."

∽

It was as they were leaving, feeling full and happy that he saw the Pontiac, lurking in the shadows behind the old warehouse. A cigarette glowed brightly then faded as someone unseen behind the dark windscreen drew in a breath. His pulse began to race as he sensed the foundations of his plan crumbling slowly. But how….?

The realisation came to him with a crippling blow that made his head swim. Distraught, he looked at Kate's face as they settled into the cab, but as she expertly gave the driver instructions on the route to her apartment, there was no sign of treachery in her sparkling eyes. She looked at him and noticed at once his hurt expression. "Hey honey, what's up?"

Sanchar ignored the pleading voice. With mounting anxiety, he remembered that he had spoken to her as to no-one in his life before. She knew too much, although even in his intimate ramblings he had not revealed the full details of his plan. He swore quietly at himself for having trusted this woman.

They spoke no words, but she sensed the chasm that had, in a second, split them apart. As the taxi pulled up outside her apartment block, she reached for his arm but he continued to gaze as if in a dream away through the opposite window. The rejection was obvious, and Kate didn't want to explore the reasons.

"Jose, I'm sorry it didn't work out," she said softly. She got out of the taxi, closed the door and disappeared behind the old revolving doors without a backward glance.

"Where to, buddy?"

He directed the driver back to his hotel, noticing that the white saloon stayed a few hundred yards or so behind. As he entered reception, he asked the young girl to give him an early call, and took the lift up to his room. Carefully checking the corridor was clear, he walked down to the outside fire escape. Quickly and silently, he scurried down into the rear yard. Fifteen minutes later, he was scaling the wall that led into the rear exit of Kate's apartment block.

Dillinger urgently shook his companion. King yawned and looked at his watch. It was a quarter to five and the sky was just beginning to brighten from the east. Dillinger shook him again, and pointed towards the hotel entrance. Grumbling King sat up, but the sight of Sanchar putting his last suitcase into the back of a waiting taxi had him awake in an instant. "Christ, he's leaving. Pete, get into the hotel and see if you can find out what the hell he's doing."

Dillinger returned panting two minutes later. "He ordered the taxi for Kennedy and told the broad behind the desk that he was flying back to Argentina. Something about a problem back at his base."

"OK. Come on, let's get round to Kate's and see if she knows anything. We can catch him up, no problem."

King was uneasy as they entered the apartment block. The protests of the sleepy night porter were soon quietened by the CIA identity card, but King's foreboding grew when Kate refused to answer her phone. Insisting on the porter breaking out the emergency key, they raced upstairs and with his hands shaking, King forced the key into the lock.

Kate's lifeless body was spread across the white rug in the hallway. A trickle of blood spread from her mouth across her white neck and onto the floor.

"Shit," King swore, swallowing hard to control the nausea that was threatening to choke him. He walked over to the phone and called reception. "Miss Jensen has been murdered. Call the local police and tell them to bring an ambulance." Despite the fury he felt, his voice was calm and full of authority. The porter hurried to co-operate. Dillinger was now sitting on the floor shaking his head in disbelief.

"How the hell ... we watched that bastard in and out of his hotel."

"Yeah. The cunning son-of-a-bitch must have realised we were behind him. Christ, what an alibi. The CIA saw me go back to my hotel and watched over me all night, your Honour," he mimicked in a Latin American accent. "Pete, get down to the car and call Langley. See if they can confirm that Sanchar is going to Buenos Aires. I hope we can nail that bastard. Move, Pete!"

King spent five minutes looking around the apartment for any record of the events of several hours before. Perhaps she had written something down for the debriefing in the morning. But if she had it was nowhere obvious. In the distance he heard the wail of the police car sirens approaching. He stepped across Kate's body and directed the two uniformed policemen who bumped into him as he walked down the corridor.

Outside at the car, Dillinger had the engine running and was shouting out of the open window "Gerry, get in quick. He's booked on the six thirty American Airlines flight to Buenos Aires. We should just catch him. The FBI are on their way right now." Realising they were now nearly thirty minutes behind Sanchar, Dillinger drove with a ferocity that surprised even King.

"Steady, Pete," he exclaimed in alarm as they sped between two crossing cars against a steady red traffic light.

Dillinger looked at him with wild eyes. "Gerry, I'm not going to let that bastard get away with what he did to Kate. She was a brave kid, and her face..." His voice broke.

"OK, OK. Just make sure we get to the airport in one piece."

When they arrived, there were already three police cars outside the entrance to the departure lounge. Joining ranks with two FBI men who kept shouting for more details, they ran across to the American Airlines desk.

"Police," King lied, but it certainly caught the startled girl's attention. "Sanchar, Jose. Has he checked in yet for Buenos Aires?"

"One moment sir. No, Mr Sanchar has not yet checked in, but he has booked a Buenos Aires seat."

King turned to the FBI men. "He's hiding out here somewhere. Let's cover the exits in case he's seen us. If he shows up, give us a call, OK?" The girl at the desk nodded.

Ten minutes later, King was getting anxious. It was six fifteen and the last call for the flight had already been made. "Let's go and see if he's managed to get through to the boarding gate," he suggested. With two uniformed policemen, they barged their way through protesting passengers and raced up to Gate Fourteen. The astonished American Airlines representative confirmed that Sanchar had not yet arrived. Confused, they looked around, but the waiting area was empty except for two coloured cleaners.

"Let's go and take a look on board," said King realising that he was clutching at straws. "We've got to look," he pleaded with the FBI officer. "OK, but let's make it quick. This plane takes off in five minutes."

An irate senior steward grudgingly allowed them on the aircraft, threatening claims for damages if they had to take off late. Slowly, they walked down the rows of the vast Boeing 747, scanning the inquisitive faces on either side. As they reached the tail section, it was obvious that Sanchar was not on board.

"He could have seen us and made off before we got properly organised," one of the policeman suggested. "If he's still here, we'll get him. If he's not, we've had it. No court in the world is going to extradite an Argentinean military officer when the CIA can confirm his alibi!"

King cursed and punched the palm of his left hand with a clenched fist in frustration. "Come on, Pete", he spat out wearily, "I need a drink."

∞

Aer Lingus 514 to Dublin and London had passed five thousand feet when the seat belt signs extinguished. There was a series of clicks as passengers relaxed and a dark haired, impeccable hostess busied herself with a silver tray.

"Coffee sir?" she asked in a soft Irish brogue.

Sanchar opened his eyes. His head was throbbing and his stomach was tied in knots. Only the thought of his Brother's dying eyes helped to shake off the image of Kate in her death throes. "Yes please," he replied, "and could you get me a large whiskey - Irish please."

CHAPTER 9

THE Hotel Veruna was shabby. The entrance hall was littered with ill-matching old furniture, and drab and dusty potted plants drooped their parched leaves towards the threadbare carpet. Feeling bewildered and exhausted, Sanchar dropped his cases heavily alongside the reception desk, raising a cloud of dust. A sleepy head appeared from the kitchen area, and with obvious reluctance the yawning manager followed and lurched towards him. Like his hotel he was old and scruffy.

"Can I help you sir?"

"Sanchar. A room for the night please."

"Ah yes, Mr Sanchar, we have your booking. Just one night wasn't it?" He thumbed his way through the coffee stained register.

Sanchar nodded and added impatiently, "Could I go straight to my room please. I'm feeling very tired."

Refusing to be hurried, the manager turned the register towards Sanchar and handed him a well-chewed biro. "Fill this in please sir," he asked, wiping his nose with the biro. Sanchar pulled his own pen from an inside pocket and entered the details in as illegible a hand as he could manage.

"Ah, Argentina. We don't get many Argentineans here," the manager noted and smiled greasily in anticipation of more information. Realising none was forthcoming, he sighed and passed over a large rusty key. "Room 13, first floor, breakfast at seven thirty."

Sanchar struggled up the narrow staircase and bundled his luggage into the tiny room ahead of him. It looked clean enough. It certainly wasn't the sort of place that would attract attention which, he supposed, was why it had been selected. He could put up with it for one night. Digging into his cabin bag he extracted the litre bottle of duty free whisky from the smaller of the two bags, and half filled the grimy tumbler from the wash basin. He downed the glass in one swallow and refilled it at once. Sighing, he got out of his clothes and sat on the single bed, his bare back against the cold plaster of the wall. After the last few days he felt very tired and not a little apprehensive. Perhaps this was not surprising, he reflected. It was a strange country to him, and he had no idea what, if anything, to expect. Optimistically, he had booked a return flight via Madrid for the following afternoon, but he had not the faintest idea whether or not he could complete his business in such a short time. He was just starting to nod off after a third whisky when he heard a slight noise at the door and leapt out of bed, wide awake. A slip of paper had been pushed under the door. He had to squint at the note to make out the barely readable pencil script. There was an address in the centre of Dublin and a time: seven o'clock.

He had just one and a half hours. Instinctively he reached again for the whisky, but some old disciplinary voice inside his head shouted a word of caution. He looked across the room at the cracked mirror on the chipboard dressing table, and was astonished at the haggard, drawn face that looked back at him with old, bloodshot eyes. It would take a long time to shake off the terrible events of New York. He was a sensitive man, a man who could not get emotionally close to people for long. But he was imbued with a strong, somewhat old-fashioned sense of chivalry and Kate's dying eyes continued to haunt him. He remembered her words; she was falling in love with him. It had been a long time since...... Sanchar clenched his fists and tried to clear his mind. He would have to pull himself together if his mission stood any chance of success. Taking a deep breath, he unpacked only what he needed for the night. After finding the right adaptor for his electric razor, he shaved meticulously and, across the corridor from his room, took a cold bath.

Glad to get out of the hotel, he found a small, surprisingly elegant tea-room across the road where he drank two cups of coffee and enjoyed his first proper meal since leaving New York. It was only a ham salad, but he felt much the better for it, and with relief he realised that he would now be able to get through the next few days. The young girl behind the till smiled cheerfully back at him as he paid the bill and left a handsome tip. To his pleasure, he felt her eyes go up and down his back as he left. Maybe he would enjoy Ireland after all. Outside, a light drizzle was falling, and the small cobblestones were slippery underfoot. A taxi responded to his wave, but he noticed that the ruddy-faced driver was less than enthusiastic when he heard the destination.

"Have you there in ten minutes, sir," he assured Sanchar in a rich Irish brogue. "But it's not much of a place for a gentleman, if you don't mind my saying so."

Sanchar ignored the remark, sat back in the deep leather seat, and gazed out with interest at the fascinating variety of people who jostled together in the evening rush hour. He had always lived close to his work as a naval pilot, and had never needed to travel far on a daily basis. Yet here, he reflected, there were several thousands of worker bees buzzing back to their various lives outside the capital. And they seemed a happy lot. Perhaps it was the whiskey.

The taxi turned into a dark, slate-grey street which looked barely inhabited. The driver slowed down and hugged the kerbside as he squinted at the numbers of the large, terraced Victorian homes. "There you are, sir, number ten. Are you sure that's the right address?"

Sanchar confirmed that it was, and hoped that the generous tip would assuage the man's curiosity and dull his memory. They bid each other good night affably, and in obvious haste the taxi driver drove off and disappeared quickly down a side street.

Sanchar took a deep breath and approached the large oak door cautiously. He knocked once before realising that it was slightly ajar. Inside a dim light beckoned him into the hallway. Hardly had he stepped inside than the light went out, leaving him in total darkness. Rough hands seized him from both sides and a thick, coarsely woven bag was thrown over his head and drawn tightly around his neck. He knew better than to resist, and in total silence he was bundled outside and thrown unceremoniously into the back of a large vehicle. As they sped off into the night, he slid around the floor and bumped from one wall to another. Straining his ears, he picked up sounds of heavy traffic outside and faintly heard the strains of music from a juke-box as they passed by a cafe. Much as he tried to remember the left and right turns, he was soon disorientated and gave up any hope of retracing the route.

After what seemed an age, the vehicle pulled off the main road, and judging by the bumps and lurches, they drove down a rough track. The vehicle stopped quickly, awkwardly throwing him sideways. As he straightened himself, the rear doors were opened and he was guided down the steps. Gruff Irish voices warned him to watch out as they crossed hilly ground. They entered a building and he heard two doors slam shut behind his faltering steps before he was pushed down onto a hard stool. It went very quiet, and he could feel perspiration breaking out all over his body as his ears strained in vain for some sound.

Without any warning, the bag was dragged off his head and a sharp light startled his dark-accustomed eyes. After blinking a couple of times, his vision slowly cleared, and he saw that he was facing a table from which glared a large white spotlight. Behind the table sat three figures, but he could make out no details save to note that the one on the right was completely bald. They waited for a few minutes before the man in the centre of the group spoke softly.

"You seem to be very keen to meet us, Captain Sanchar." He didn't wait for an answer. "What makes you think you have anything that might be of interest to our movement?"

Sanchar tried to sit upright. His voice seemed distant and strange to him. "I explained my purpose for wishing to see you in New York and..."

"Captain Sanchar," interrupted the man again, obviously the spokesman, "all we have heard so far is one bloody silly story about you wanting to settle an old score with the British. We know all about your brother, so don't give us any bullshit. What exactly do you have in mind, Captain?"

Sanchar took a deep breath and without concealing anything, revealed his full plan. When he had finished, the spokesman let out a long whistle. "So what do you want of us?" he asked after a couple of minutes.

"I can't guarantee finding the right ship," admitted Sanchar. "There will be a lot of small boats around the harbour entrance to Montevideo, and I must have some way of identifying the Queen's Yacht at long range. As it stands, it could be anywhere within fifty miles with the navigation equipment on my aircraft, and I won't have the fuel to search that sort of area."

The tree men waited in silence. Sanchar took a deep breath. " Now, if you could get a small transmitting device on board, I could use my aircraft equipment to home in on the Yacht. I know it's a tall order but…"

The room went silent as the three pondered the implications of Sanchar's plan. "And who else knows about this, Captain?" asked a voice from the left.

"No-one. This is the first time I have spoken a word about it."

"What about the girl you murdered in New York?"

Sanchar nearly fell off the stool. How on earth had they found out about Kate so quickly? "She was an informant, but she didn't have any of the details. She got in the way."

"You're certainly a determined man, Captain, I'll give you that," chuckled the bald man in obvious admiration. He was silenced by a sideways look from the leading spokesman, who then turned back to Sanchar. "Just stay where you are."

The three left unseen through a door behind the light, but Sanchar was aware of at least two men standing in the darkness behind him. He asked for a cigarette, but got no reply. After nearly an hour he was given a plastic cup of water, but he could see only the hand of the man who passed it from behind him. He sensed that he would be safer not seeing any faces. It was another tense hour before the door finally opened and the three returned. There was obvious antagonism between them, and he noticed that the man with the bald head was breathing heavily. There had clearly been one hell of a row.

"Captain Sanchar," announced the man in the centre", "you have posed us quite a dilemma." His voice was hoarse, and Sanchar could see that his hands were shaking. "We would like to help our Argentinean friends in anything associated with their efforts to decolonise the Malvinas Islands. You suffer the same banditry of your rightful land as do we in the North." Sanchar nodded hopefully. "However, this is obviously a personal vendetta, and without support of your military colleagues we see little possibility of you succeeding. And we do not wish to be associated with a disastrous failure. Frankly, Captain, you are going a bit too far for our purposes, and even if you succeed, I'm not sure we could justify this particular outrage with our .... with our supporters." He sneered as he spoke. "There are too many people around the World who see the British Monarchy through rose tinted glasses."

He sighed and Sanchar just caught the outline of his hard features as he leaned forward and stared at him intently. "I'm sorry, Captain Sanchar, but you're on your own."

He nodded once to the unseen man behind, and as he did so Sanchar was hit on the base of the skull. A shower of sparks exploded in front of his eyes, and as he slumped forward dizzily, he felt a sharp prick at the back of his neck. Slowly he drifted into unconsciousness.

∞

"Mr Sanchar! Mr Sanchar!" a distant voice called out. He opened his eyes and after a few dizzy seconds realised he was in his bed in the hotel. "Mr Sanchar, are you there sir?" Groaning, he struggled to his feet, pulled the bedcover round himself and opened the door. The red-faced manager was panting outside. "Oh there you are sir. There's a man on the phone for you. Says it's long distance and urgent."

"I'll be down right away. Tell him to wait," replied the still groggy Sanchar, wondering who on earth knew where he was.

He dragged on his trousers and a shirt, and pushed his feet into the shoes which had been thrown into a corner. All his clothes stank of whiskey, he noticed as he rushed down to the entrance hall. The manager was waiting to take him to the wooden telephone booth, which was adorned with the efforts of years of graffiti. Sanchar closed the door tightly and stared at the manager until he went away.

"Hello" he said cautiously. "Hello." The line was dead. Sanchar shrugged and replaced the receiver. Shaking his fuzzy head, he climbed the stairs back to his room. After a shower, he found his way down a road to a pokey cafe and ordered a coffee.

"By Jove, sir, you look as though you hung one on last night," the waiter chuckled. Sanchar nodded. He sipped the scolding coffee. It was dreadful. Why couldn't anyone in this country make coffee? As he put the cup down, he noticed his hand was trembling. It was all coming apart. Without the homing device there was no hope of finding his target in the open sea. He cursed. The sound of his own voice made him jump. Christ, he was in a mess. Best to give it all up and go home. He paid his bill and went back to the hotel.

The manager rushed up to meet him. "Mr Sanchar, it's that fellah on the phone again."

Sanchar pushed him out of the way. He picked up the phone. "Hello," he whispered, watching the manager skulking just a few yards away. "Sanchar?"

"Yes, who is this?"

"You don't need to know." The voice was mid European, German perhaps. "I understand from a friend in the Irish Republican movement that you want a certain piece of equipment left in a convenient place for a mutual friend?"

Sanchar was appalled. How did this man get such information? "Sanchar, did you hear me?"

"Yes, yes. Exactly who told you this?"

"You ask too many questions for a man who needs so much help. Captain, we can do this job for you, but it won't be easy for us .... or cheap for you. Are you still interested?"

Sanchar's mind was a blank, muddled by the events of the night before. "Captain, I'm ringing off."

"No, no, wait," shouted Sanchar.

"Alright, are you interested then?"

"How much will it cost?"

"Twenty five thousand US dollars, to be paid into a numbered Swiss account before activation of the equipments." Sanchar forced himself to think.

"Yes, I can do that." He wasn't absolutely sure that he could raise that much, but he had to seize the situation now and sort the money out later.

"Good," the voice replied brightly. "Now take note of this number. It is Account Number 09956023 at Credit Allemagne in Zurich. Got it?"

"Yes, but how do I know you'll deliver?"

"You don't. But if we fail to deliver the equipment, you will receive your money back. And don't worry, Captain, you have a very good ally in Ireland and we don't like to upset him. It's very bad for business. Do you accept?"

"Yes," Sanchar replied. He had no other option.

"Good. Now I need to know exactly when you want the equipment activated. Because of the small size, it will operate for a maximum of four hours, and probably for less in a cold climate. For obvious reasons, it would not be a good idea to start it earlier than absolutely necessary."

He was right. "Agreed. At half past three in the afternoon Buenos Aires time, on May the second. That is zero seven thirty hours Greenwich Mean Time."

There was a slight pause. "I've got that. Now don't be tempted to try and cheat us, Captain Sanchar. If the money has not been delivered by start of work on the first of May, we shall alert the British Foreign Office and blow your whole plan. Do you understand?"

"Yes." The phone went dead. Still feeling baffled, Sanchar slowly replaced the receiver in its cradle and pulled open the stiff wooden door. His mind was racing, despair now turned to hope. But who....? It came to him suddenly, that the man with the bald head must have been involved, but he would never know for sure.

"Everything alright, sir?" questioned the manager hopefully.

"Yes, thank you," Sanchar replied gruffly. He looked at his watch. It was nearly nine o'clock and his time in this country was running out.

"Order me a taxi for the airport at twelve o'clock will you."

"Very good sir," the manager made a note in his pad. "A fine state you were in last night sir," he chuckled, winking mischievously. "I'm glad you had friends to look after you, I'm sure." He laughed out loud as Sanchar climbed the stairs. In the seclusion of his room, he found himself trembling with excitement. It was coming together at last: a live Exocet, a homing device and an unsuspecting quarry!

Sanchar was not sorry to be leaving Dublin. It was full of whispering undercurrents that he didn't understand, and the richly accented English was difficult on his ears. He yearned for his home at Puerto Belgrano, and for the warmth of Sabina's nakedness. The thought of a woman's body brought his mind back to Kate Jensen. He shook his head to rid himself of her image. The taxi screeched to a halt outside the airport departures entrance. It was still raining.

"There you are sir, nicely on time. Three punts please."

Sanchar paid off the taxi driver and entered the modern looking terminal. Following his usual suspicion of porters, he declined their advances, but took advantage of a luggage trolley. He returned the check-in desk attendant's forced smile, but failed to notice her imperceptible nod, as he moved off towards the departure gate.

Without warning a heavy hand fell on his shoulder. "Captain Sanchar?" He turned round and found himself facing a large, burly man in a three-piece tweed suit. His face was deep red, and his breath came in short wheezes from a fleshy mouth. Two armed policemen in uniform stood behind him.

"Come with me please, sir," he insisted, taking hold of Sanchar's right arm firmly. Sanchar realised that there was no point in arguing.

He was taken via a long bare corridor to a small, smoke-filled office. Behind a desk sat two men in dark suits, and just out of sight to his left, he could make out a third sitting quietly in the corner. "Mr Sanchar, I am Superintendent Stevens of the British Special Branch, and this is Inspector O'Connell of the Irish Garda."

"What am I doing here?" protested Sanchar, if only to give some impression of innocent outrage.

His question was ignored. "Captain, what are you doing here in Ireland?"

"I am on holiday for a couple of weeks, and I wanted to visit Dublin," he replied indignantly. "What is so unusual about that? Is this how you treat your visitors to Ireland?"

There was a snort. "Strange holiday, Captain. You only arrived yesterday and you're leaving already. Didn't you like the climate?" O'Connell asked sarcastically. Sanchar didn't reply. After a minute, Stevens raised his eyes again. "Where did you stay last night?"

"The Hotel Veruna"

"What do you know of a lady called Kate Jensen?" This came as a blow but he managed to stay cool.

"I met her in New York and took her to dinner. That's all, why?"

"She's dead ..... murdered, Captain Sanchar."

Sanchar was ready this time and made a good job of appearing shocked. "My God, how?"

"Strangled," replied Stevens. "When did you last see her?"

"The night before last. I took her back to her apartment block. She told me not to bother seeing her inside. And then I went straight back to my hotel in the taxi."

"Did you leave the hotel again?"

"No, I had a very early start and so went straight to bed. The receptionist will confirm that I didn't leave the hotel again that night."

"Yes. We've already checked, Captain," O'Connell said acidly. Sanchar almost smiled.

The door behind him opened and unseen by Sanchar, a man shook his head to Stevens. He had no doubt that they had searched his luggage, but had found nothing that would justify arrest. "You may go, Captain Sanchar," sighed Stevens with obvious exasperation.

"My baggage....?"

"Will be on the aircraft."

Sanchar turned to go. As he did so the man who had been sitting quietly in the corner stood up and faced him, eye to eye. "Goodbye, Captain Sanchar, I do hope we meet again."

Sanchar looked down at the large identification card clipped to the man's lapel. "Goodbye, Mr Turnbull. I hope we do not."

They were to do so, but in circumstances that neither of them could ever have imagined.

CHAPTER 10

Sir Michael Townsend leaned back in his soft leather rotating chair. He looked exasperated. Patiently, he repeated his question. "But Richard, what are you asking me to do? All you've got so far is a man with a grudge who seems to be flapping around trying to cause trouble." He sighed irritably, and banged his hand down on the mahogany desk.

"Look, he's been to New York, may, I repeat may, have killed some girl who pushed her luck too far, and then tries to make contact with the IRA. From what you have gathered, and you admit yourself from a very dodgy source, the IRA told him to get on his bike and go back to Argentina, which is precisely what he's done. Right? So what can he do now? Even if he had planned to get a bomb on the Royal Yacht, he's obviously given up. And as the Yacht is sailing tomorrow, he's blown any chances of trying again. We've already gone over the chances of him getting on board in Rio or Montevideo. There's no way. With only one gangplank for most of the time, and that closely guarded, he'd have to come disguised as Prince Philip!"

Turnbull still looked worried. He shook his head and gesticulated with both hands. "I'm sorry, but I just don't like it, sir. I know it sounds thin, but when I looked him in the eye, he didn't look like a man staring defeat in the face. He looked bloody arrogant to me." He rotated his coffee mug in his hand a few times. "Perhaps he's going to try and get a mine in the water, or maybe attach something to the hull. I just don't know."

"It won't work, Richard. There will be lookouts constantly on watch for frogman activity, and the hull will be thoroughly searched by our own divers at irregular intervals, but never less than every twelve hours. As I told you, HMS Cornwall has been designated for escort duties, and she'll be keeping a careful watch. You're worrying too much."

"I suppose you're right," admitted Turnbull wearily, "but I'd feel a lot better if I could be around when the Queen's on board."

"Ah, now I see." Townsend said slyly. "You fancy a couple of weeks in the sun, eh? Fancy an exotic Brazilian beauty, do we?"

Turnbull ignored the remark and continued to stare across the desk. Townsend sighed in resignation. "Alright, alright, if it'll get you out of my hair you can fly out to Rio and do some sniffing around before the Queen arrives."

"And Montevideo?"

"OK and Montevideo. But I want you on Cornwall and not on the Yacht herself. We don't want the Royal household getting the jitters, do we? And let's keep this low key. I'll have a quiet word with the Home Secretary and leave it to him to decide who else to tell. But don't you go frightening anybody. Understood? Now off you go, I've got work to do."

Turnbull returned to his poky office, where Superintendent Stevens was helping himself to a cup of instant coffee. "Well?" he enquired.

"He thinks I'm getting in a state about nothing. He

may well be right. Anyway, he's agreed that I can join Cornwall before the Queen arrives in Rio, and stay with the party until the visit to Montevideo is over. I'm not sure what the hell I'm going to do down there, but I'll be sitting on the edge of my seat if I stay here. What about you Mike? Do you want to come back to Southampton with me tonight?"

"No, to be honest, I'd feel a real idiot looking over Hemsby's shoulder again. They've got it all sewn up. There's nothing more we can do."

Turnbull sucked his teeth and thought for a moment. "I know you're right, but I think I'll drive down and watch her leave tomorrow. I've got nothing else to do this weekend."

"I don't know how you can work up there like that. I always get dizzy standing on a bar stool," chuckled the naval policeman.

The carpenter smiled from his precarious position on top of the twenty-foot light alloy ladder. "You just hang on to the ladder, mate," he called down. "I've nearly finished."

He completed the change of the large round wooden stay at the bottom end of the flagpole that would hold the Royal Ensign. "There, that's better. Should last a few months. These bloody things are always cracking."

He slithered down the ladder and stood for a moment admiring his handiwork. Nodding in satisfaction at a good job done, he pulled a packet of cigarettes out of his dark blue overalls and offered one to the policeman. "Thanks, mate. Fancy a cup of tea before you go?"

"Thanks very much. I'm off to Pompey so a nice cuppa would be just to ticket."

As they left the ship, he let the policeman get a few

paces ahead, stopped and looked back at the flagpole. Smiling, he nodded with satisfaction ... yes, that should do the trick.

∞

Turnbull kept in the background as much as he could. He felt totally superfluous, as the Navy went about the business of seeing the Royal Yacht safely out to sea. There she would join her sleek escort, HMS Cornwall, a Type 22 Frigate.

Lieutenant Commander Hemsby moved alongside him and let out a long sigh as the Yacht slowly moved off her moorings. "She looks magnificent, doesn't she?" His voice reflected the pride felt by every seaman when he sees a beautiful ship putting to sea.

Turnbull had to agree. "I sometimes wish I'd joined the Navy," he replied wistfully. "My father was a sailor. He served on minesweepers during the war. It's in the blood, I suppose, but getting married early in life put paid to that fantasy."

He reflected ruefully on how events had turned against him. He should have joined that Navy after all.

"When are you flying out?" Hemsby enquired.

"Not for ten days yet. The boss seems to think I'm just after a bit of skirt on Ipanema beach."

Hemsby sniggered." You be careful out there. The girls look lovely, but they can give you diseases that haven't even been given a name yet."

"Yes, I'll be careful," he replied absent-mindedly.

∞

Sanchar had slept for nearly eighteen hours, but he still felt exhausted. He'd already alarmed his PA with an uncharacteristic irritability, and the news that the trial aircraft radars had not been fully checked out yet had sent him into a fury. When the worst of his rage had subsided, he had sent for Commanders Mantana and Aries. They were now awaiting his summons in the outer office, whilst he sat quietly and tried to compose himself. He knew he had come close to his personal limits during the past week, and he had no doubt that if he was going to get through the next fortnight, he would have to keep himself under better control. He raised his coffee shakily to his lips, took a deep breath and pressed the buzzer through to his PA.

Aries and Mantana came in, saluted and remained standing. They looked nervous. Mantana broke the silence. "I hope you had a good leave sir," he asked lamely.

"I did, thank you. In fact I was feeling very refreshed until I heard that the trial on the new jamming pod had been delayed. I thought I made it absolutely clear that I would accept no excuses for not getting the trial off on time." He looked at them expectantly.

Aries coughed. "Er, yes sir. I'm afraid we ran into a few problems. But we should be OK for a start first thing tomorrow morning."

"Not good enough, Aries," Sanchar said emphatically. "This trial is vital, and if we don't produce the results on time, heads will roll. The Admiral has already been on the phone asking why we can't start today," he lied.

It had the desired effect. Both men looked shocked. "We have a little slack in the timetable, sir," Mantana added brightly. "I know we can make up the time."

Sanchar ignored the remark. "I have been given information that the British are flying more than the average reconnaissance missions out of the Malvinas." This was also a lie. "The Admiral suggests that we look for a quiet period for the trial firing, so we'll plan for May the second, which is a Saturday. If I get airborne about three o'clock, that should be about right."

The two commanders looked uncomfortable. "The men won't be happy about working over the weekend," Aries complained.

"Well I'm sorry but that's for you to sort out," Sanchar replied acidly. "I suggest you get on with your work, gentlemen. Oh, Mantana," he added, "Don't forget I want to get airborne a couple of times this week."

"We have you down to fly on Wednesday and Friday, sir," Mantana replied, hoping to make up some lost ground.

As they left, Sanchar leaned back in his chair and closed his eyes. So far he was just about keeping to the plan, but he was more than a little concerned about the strange telephone call. Who was it? And who had set it all up? Yes, probably the bald man ... As time was obviously short, he had been to see his bank manager the minute he had set foot back on Argentinean soil. In vain, the bemused man had advised Sanchar against the sale of his entire portfolio of shares, most of which were profitably invested in Japanese and European companies. To his very pleasant surprise, the sale had netted nearly $32,000, more than enough for his purposes, and the money should be in the Swiss Account within days. It could all, of course, be a confidence trick. He had to rely on the honour of thieves and he wouldn't know for sure until he switched on his electronic homing device on May the second. His heart fluttered. Twelve days; twelve days before he had the chance he had been waiting for these last ten years. And who were these people? He was a fool to trust them. The pencil he was holding snapped in his grip.

∞

Ralph Prentice sat nervously on the wooden bench. He had been waiting for nearly two hours, but this didn't surprise him in the least. In Argentina, you got used to waiting, unless of course you were prepared to pay handsomely for the privilege of a timely hearing. He was not, or rather his masters in Langley were not. This was going to be difficult meeting. Relations with Argentina had never been better, but the civilian police did not like the CIA, and although Prentice was formally on the economic staff, most of his contacts knew his real role in life.

Certainly the man for whom he had wasted most of his Tuesday morning knew exactly what he was doing in Argentina. But Inspector Rosario was an unusual man. Fat, sensual and unusually vicious, he seemed to have a finger in every pie in Buenos Aires, and he was feared by innocent and guilty alike. He had been a non-commissioned officer in the Army during the bad days, but he had been too unpredictable even for the Army, and had been eased out following a spate of barely concealed atrocities.

Prentice was just about to light up another cigarette, when the door opened and an anorexic young police officer stuck his head out. "Senor Prentice?" Ralph nodded. "The Inspector will see you now."

Rosario seemed engrossed in papers in front of him. After standing awkwardly for a while, Prentice decided to sit down in the large old leather chair in front of the desk. It was a mistake, as a large spring half poked out from the thin covering on the seat and made him feel extremely uncomfortable.

However, he needed to establish the right relationship with this man, so he would have to live with the discomfort. Rosario put down his pen, ran a blotter across a piece of paper, and then finally looked up at Prentice. "So, how is the United States of America's economic adviser?" he asked with a sneer.

"Well, thank you, Inspector. I trust you are not as unhealthy as you look"

Rosario looked angry for a few seconds, but then burst into a loud grating laugh. He pulled out a long Havana cigar from his inside pocket, bit the end off with tobacco stained teeth, and lit up amidst clouds of dark smoke. "So", he said eventually, "you want to know something about Captain Sanchar of the Armada, eh?"

Prentice nodded and leaned forward in his seat. The spring stuck in further.

"Hmm. Why have you come to me? I do not know this man. You should go and see someone in the Ministry of Defence."

"I don't want to cause trouble with the Navy. Frankly, it's a long shot, and if I took it to some Admiral they'd only close ranks and throw me out. I've seen it before."

"You may yet be thrown out of here my friend," Rosario joked, pointing his cigar at Prentice. "Tell me, why you are so interested in Captain Sanchar?"

Prentice gave him the bare facts, omitting some details of the IRA's involvement, and saying only that Sanchar was suspected of planning some disruption to the Queen's visit to South America.

Rosario looked incredulous. "I think you're mad, senor. Why should anyone in Argentina try to cause trouble with the British now? Our governments have been good friends for some years, and the President has declared publicly that any progress towards regaining our birthright must be secured by diplomatic means only. You are surely, as you say in your country, barking up the wrong tree." He looked pleased with himself.

"I'm sure you're right, Inspector," Prentice admitted, "but we are concerned that the Queen's visit to Brazil and Uruguay should go ahead without incident, and ..."

Rosario interrupted him with a sharp bang of his fist on the desk. Prentice jumped. "I couldn't give a shit about the British Queen, the Brazilians or the Uruguayans. I've got too much on my plate to be chasing around following up every intrigue the CIA sniffs out. And I warn you, Mr Prentice, if you start meddling around in my area, you will be very sorry. That is all I have to say to you."

Feeling shaken, Prentice left, and was glad to get away from the stifling, intimidating atmosphere in the Police Headquarters. Inside Rosario clicked on his intercom. "Send Sergeant Hugo through to me ... now!"

Hugo arrived within two minutes. He was in sharp contrast to Rosario: thin, closely cropped hair and weasel-like. But like his boss he oozed violence. "You heard all that?" Hugo nodded.

"Get a couple of your men to keep a watch on Sanchar, but tell them that if he gets rattled and causes trouble for me, I'll cut off their noses. And you do some digging around and see what you can find out. I don't like it Hugo, and I do not want any trouble here. It will be bad for us all. Let me know if you come up with anything interesting."

Hugo nodded and left. He was a man of few words, but Rosario knew that if Sanchar was planning anything, he would be found out. He opened the file in front of him and stared at Sanchar's photograph. "Don't give me any trouble, Captain Sanchar," he said, tapping the photograph with his cigar. "No, don't give me any trouble or you will be very, very sorry."

CHAPTER 11

∞

"Rim, no damage."

Squadron Leader Des Browne cursed under his breath, eased back on the throttles and repositioned his Tornado F3 fighter six feet behind the refuelling basket. Dominating his vision was the under-fuselage of the Tristar, which was providing the fuel to get the three fighters down to Ascension Island. The lonely staging post in the middle of the Atlantic Ocean would give them a chance to rest before their onward flight to the Falkland Islands.

"Nine o'clock at six inches," called his navigator in the rear seat. Flight Lieutenant Mike Curtis used the clock code to indicate where the refuelling probe had nudged back the basket as it swung out in the airflow. Browne stabilised his aircraft and waited for the hose assembly to settle down. Now was the time when an inexperienced pilot, embarrassed by failing to make contact on the first approach, would rush into a second attempt, invariably missing yet again. But Browne had been flying fighters for twenty years, and he knew that he must bide his time. Readjusting his visual references on the fuselage of the Tristar, he slowly accelerated the two or three knots required to ensure that when the probe engaged the basket, it did so with just the right amount of force. To make contact with too much speed could cause damage, which would inevitably result in a return to the United Kingdom or a diversion into Western Africa. Too soft a contact would fail to activate the locking mechanism that enabled fuel to flow from the mother aircraft to the receiver.

"Left slightly," Curtis advised, as again the approaching bulk of the Tornado's nose forced the gaping drogue out to the left. With a satisfying clunk the probe engaged the basket. Connection completed, the precious fuel began to flow into the half-empty tanks. For the next twenty minutes, Browne concentrated on maintaining the correct position in behind the Tristar. It was physically and mentally demanding, and by the time the tanker captain gave him permission to break contact, he was feeling exhausted.

"Ascension here we come," called out Curtis jubilantly. They had completed their last refuelling bracket, and could now accelerate away from the Tristar towards Wideawake Airfield. Together the three sleek grey aircraft swept back their wings, increased thrust to full power, and sped away from the cumbersome tanker aircraft at the speed of sound.

An hour later, Curtis was relieved to see Ascension Island come into view. There was no sign of storm activity, which would have meant a prolonged holding period, and even a further refuelling from one of the tankers kept on the island to cope with a sudden weather deterioration. So distant from any mainland, it would be unthinkable to divert to another airfield. Fortunately, experience had shown that squalls and storms, although common, tended to be of short duration, and a prudent reserve of fuel to hold off for a while was considered sufficient precautionary action.

Lining up on the main runway, Browne called the other two fighters into close formation and executed one low pass across the airfield before turning downwind to land. As he lowered his undercarriage, he reflected on how barren this coke-strewn island looked, but how important it had become as a staging post for aircraft and ships forming the continuous trail down to the South Atlantic.

As they taxied into the bright concrete dispersal, Browne was pleased to see the Squadron Engineering officers snapping open cans of cold lager for the six thirsty aircrew. Gratefully, he eased himself out of the cockpit, reflecting, not for the first time, that these nine hour sorties were taking a greater toll on his body as he grew older. No matter, a few cold beers, a hot bath, and then a spell lounging on the artificial beach would soon soothe his aching bones.

After slaking his raging thirst, Browne completed the necessary post-sortie paperwork and gathered the aircrews around him in the operations room. "Good work, gentlemen, but that's the easy bit. I've just taken a quick look at the forecast for Mount Pleasant tomorrow. If what they say is right, the Falklands could well be in for some rough weather. So let's take it easy today, get to bed early tonight and be up for a briefing at six o'clock local time."

One of the younger officers stirred. "Sir, when are we getting a briefing? We're all feeling a bit in the dark at the moment."

"I appreciate that, Tony," Browne replied. "Now that we're away from the UK media, I don't suppose it will do any harm for you to have the basic details, but you'll have to wait for a full briefing from the MOD project officer when we arrive at Mount Pleasant. For now, you'll have read in the newspapers that the Queen is visiting Rio and Montevideo next week. Well, we're going to provide top cover over the Yacht as she sails down into Uruguayan waters. There's going to be a Nimrod on anti-submarine duties as well, but it looks as though she will be operating independently. We'll just stick to our usual job, with the Tristar providing the fuel."

"Have the Argies issued any threats?" asked another young officer. He seemed keen on the prospects of a fight.

Browne smiled. He liked to see natural aggression in the younger aircrew. "No, I'm afraid not, Kevin. As far as I can see, we're just there as a token gesture."

Their disappointment was obvious. "Come on," he chided, "I'll buy you all a beer."

***

Richard Turnbull stood rather unsteadily next to Captain David Morrison, who commanded HMS Cornwall. The Type 22 frigate looked and felt efficient. From the bridge, across the rectangular Seawolf missiles and massive Vickers 4.5 inch gun, the bow gently nosed into the choppy green waves of the Atlantic Ocean.

Slightly swept, on the starboard side, Turnbull could just make out the Royal Yacht through the light sea spray. In order to achieve her maximum range of nearly 4000 miles, the new Britannia needed to cruise at fourteen knots. Whilst this was less than half the available speed of Cornwall, the powerful escort seemed untroubled.

"Oakleaf on the nose at five miles," the young leading seaman called out from his position alongside the helmsman. The captain nodded and raised his binoculars. The Royal Fleet Auxiliary refueller, or `oiler' as the Navy prefer to call them, had been showing on the Mark 1006 Sea Surveillance Radar which glowed bright green from the console in front of the Captain's revolving seat.

He turned to Turnbull. "We should complete the rendezvous in an hour and refuelling will be complete by nightfall. I think you'll enjoy watching it."

Turnbull nodded in agreement. After nearly a week at sea he had visited every part of the ship, and had flown twice on the frigate's Lynx helicopter. Even on a fairly large ship of four thousand nine hundred tons laden, with a complement of two hundred and fifty officers and men, there was a limit to the entertainment that could be provided for a mere spectator. He admired greatly the professionalism and character of the young men who made this costly piece of fighting equipment work. They made him feel old: even the Captain was nearly five years his junior.

"Classified signal for you in the comms room," the radio operator on his right called out.

"Thanks, I'll take it now," Turnbull replied. He liked people to know he was not just there for the cruise, and the occasional signal from London helped.

In the communications centre he had been allocated a small safe for his period codes and ciphers, and a makeshift desk on which to translate the scrambled gibberish into intelligible text. Otherwise he tried to keep a low profile. Apart from Morrison, no-one on the ship really understood the reasons for his presence amongst them, and that's the way he wanted to keep it.

The message was from Sir Michael Townsend. As it slowly took shape, it did little to cheer him.

FOR TURNBULL FROM TOWNSEND STOP CIA HAVE SOUGHT ASSISTANCE FROM BUENOS AIRES POLICE IN SURVEILLANCE OF SANCHAR STOP RECEPTION MOST HOSTILE AND AGENT WARNED OFF MOST EMPHATICALLY STOP EXPECT NO FURTHER PROGRESS IN THIS AREA STOP RAF FIGHTERS AND NIMROD AIRCRAFT IN TRANSIT FALKLANDS STOP SEEMS QUIET DOESN'T IT STOP MESSAGE ENDS.

Turnbull could almost hear Townsend's sneering voice coming through the cipher. Carefully, he re-locked the codes in his safe and shredded the original text and his translated copy. He found it difficult to believe that Sanchar had given up, but what could he possibly do now? They were not stopping until Rio de Janeiro, and security there would be tight. Nevertheless, with Sanchar's movements virtually impossible to monitor, it could well be his best chance. Yes, Turnbull reflected, if he was going to take a shot at the Queen or plant a bomb, he would have to do it in Rio.

∞

"A bit rusty, sir"
Sanchar nodded. His simulator sortie had taken a lot out of him. A look in the mirror after climbing out of the machine had shown him as much. As he sipped his coffee he reflected ruefully how his operational edge had been dulled over the years. He could still fly the aircraft well, if not to perfection. But the intricacies of advanced weaponry and the myriad switch selections required during a complex mission were now beyond him. He knew he would have to work hard to regain currency in the highly demanding tactics and procedures, and this was where the simulator would prove invaluable. In the safe and well supervised environment which it provided, he would be able to practise and refine his operational skills for the big day itself. He was in no doubt that to be successful under pressure, he must be perfect in his operation of the weapons system under easy conditions.

"I'm flying a practice for the live firing later today," Sanchar said to the simulator instructor, "so I'd better sort out those procedures, especially during target acquisition. I think I need to sit down and work out how

TARGET – THE QUEEN! *Christopher Coville*

I should be making better use of the electronic jamming pod as well."

"That's right sir," the young Lieutenant agreed. "Remember that the pod will jam every radar automatically, but you have to decide the best time to dispense chaff and infra-red flare decoys. I reckon the best time is when you realise the opponent is in a firing position, or during the late stages of a bombing run over a well-defended target." Sanchar took this in as the instructor continued. "Of course, during an Exocet profile, you shouldn't get near the target at all, so your pod should only be used against any fighters that bounce you."

Sanchar nodded. "Yes, you're right. Perhaps we can look at that again in the next sortie. Let's look at a straightforward Exocet firing first, to get the switch selections and radar work sorted out. Then I'd like to do the same thing again with a fighter bounce and some defensive measures from the target."

Sanchar knew that the Royal Yacht would be escorted. He was well aware of the capabilities of the Type 22 frigate, which could use chaff, bundles of minute metal-coated plastic needles, to jam out the missile's homing radar. Moreover, she was armed with Seawolf missiles and a brace of lethal Phoenix Gatling guns, which could destroy the missile in flight. It was vital that he planned his approach with great care.

Sanchar drained his coffee, ran a hand through his damp hair, and re-fitted his flying helmet. The technician closed the opaque canopy down over the cockpit, and methodically he ran through the check list that would prepare the aircraft and its weapons system for action. Despite his fatigue, he felt more at home and was soon pulling away from the first synthetic attack.

"That's a lot better sir," crackled the instructor's voice in his headphones. "Happy to go on to the more realistic scenarios now?"

"Affirmative," replied Sanchar, and set himself up for the new profile. It was a good practice, starting with a realistic attack against him from a fighter aircraft, which he successfully deceived using the new jamming pod. As he made good his escape, he saw that the simulated surface target was obviously well-defended. The radar indicated that the primary vessel was being closely escorted, probably by a warship, but he was able to adjust his attack to ensure that the missile would go for the right target and not for the escort. He completed three simulated runs before declaring that he was content.

To his relief, so was the instructor. "Excellent, sir. That was a good workout, and you should have no problem in the air this afternoon. I hope you have a good trip."

After his usual light lunch of a sandwich in the office, Sanchar went down to the flight line, where he was met by Commander Mantana and Lieutenant Commander Aries.

Sanchar knew that the Squadron Commander would have been keeping a close check on his performance and progress in the simulator, but he was not surprised when he asked how the sortie had gone.

"I was a bit rusty on the weaponry procedures at first," he replied, "but I did another sortie and I'm a lot happier now."

"OK sir," Mantana said, clearly pleased that the simulator instructor's comments to him had not been mollified by undue courtesy to rank. "We've got your aeroplane ready, plus a spare if you need it. The fighter crews are waiting for you in the main briefing room."

Sanchar entered and after inviting the assembled group to sit down, he listened attentively while the meteorological officer gave his briefing. The weather would be good: cool, windy, but without any low cloud either at base or in the exercise area. The Mirage flight leader briefed on his planned tactics and operating area, and Sanchar concluded with an overall plan for the simulated Exocet attack on the derelict ship that served as the target.

"Any questions gentlemen? Good, let's go then, and plan for an on-task time of fifteen thirty hours local."

⌒⌒

Sanchar donned the cumbersome flying kit, picked up his helmet and strode out to the flight line. After checking the outside of the Super Etendard, he climbed in and started the engine. The aircraft throbbed gently around him, and lights flashed on and off as systems came quickly into life. After carefully aligning his navigational equipment, he taxied out and awaited the departure of the two Mirage fighters. They would go and position themselves on a combat air patrol, or CAP, some fifty miles away, somewhere between the airfield and the target.

Hopefully, using tactics, evasive navigation and the jamming pod, he would get the better of them.

The two Mirages roared off in close formation. Sanchar lined up on the runway in the shimmering heat haze left behind by their glowing reheat plumes. The Super Etendard was heavy, and even without the Exocet missile that would be fitted on the day of the trial, it seemed reluctant to leave the runway. Once he had cleared the ground, he raised the flaps and checked the engine indicators. This was a critical stage of flight, and any early warning of possible engine failure could help avert a disaster. All was well. He accelerated the aircraft to four hundred knots and settled down at two hundred feet above the rocky ground.

Two minutes later he crossed the coast and descended

to wave top level. A small flock of gulls, much feared by all low flying pilots, passed by under his port wing. One large bird ingested into the single, overworked and fragile engine would leave him struggling to sustain sufficient power to avoid stalling.

A few miles out to sea, he was startled as the radar warning receiver alarmed, indicating that one of the fighters was closing on him from the right. With their antiquated pulse radars, the Mirages would not see him at this level until they were very close. He banked his aircraft steeply and turned hard to the left. It would delay him, but after one minute he would be able to resume his original track towards the target.

He could then make up some time by accelerating fifty knots. Peering anxiously over his shoulder, he was surprised to see one of the fighters rolling in behind at about three miles. His tactic had clearly failed, but all was not lost. He was still outside missile range, and good use of both speed and the jamming pod might save him. He switched the pod to automatic and confirmed that the correct lights illuminated on the system management panel. But the fighter kept closing. Sanchar could see him clearly against the bright sky, but he knew the Mirage pilot would not yet be able to pick out the well camouflaged Super Etendard visually against the dark grey sea. His radio burst into life. "Check switches, check switches".

The pilot in the pursuing aircraft could obviously see him on radar, and wondered why the jamming pod was not affecting the system. Sanchar re-checked his switches. "Switches all set. Confirm still nothing seen?" he asked in the guarded terms agreed for security reasons.

"Nothing seen".

Sanchar swore and threw his aircraft into an emergency turn towards the fighter, which by then had closed to within lethal range. It was too late. "Good kill, good kill", the Mirage pilot called out jubilantly over the radio. For some inexplicable reason the electronic pod had failed to jam the fighter's radar. Sanchar cursed again.

"Roger, understood. Continuing with the exercise", he replied with resignation.

The fighter peeled away, his job done. Sanchar turned back towards the target, which soon appeared on his long range acquisition radar. His earlier simulator sorties proved their worth, and the final run-in and simulated weapon release went perfectly. Flushed with success, he was feeling a little better as he pulled high over the target, his vision greying as the acceleromator showed nearly four times the force of gravity. He grunted as the anti-G suit inflated, squeezing his stomach and legs.

A sudden thud shook the airframe. Sanchar's heart missed a beat. Remember the basics! Back with the control column ... now forward ... slowly, easy, gently back to level flight. Another bang! The aircraft began to vibrate violently. Red attention lamps ... the emergency alarm bell ... fly the aircraft ... above all else ... fly the aircraft ... keep it level ... keep it straight ... hold the nose up ... hold it up!

A quick look ...engine seems OK....but hydraulic pressure low ... no brakes, no approach flaps, no landing gear. Sanchar knew his life was hanging on a thin thread. Stay calm ... stay calm ... think. Checking position ... fine ... now, gently turn the aircraft towards base.

There was no problem with normal flying manoeuvres, but he would need to think carefully about how to get the aircraft back safely on the ground. He would have no flaps, which enabled the wings to produce more lift on the approach, and so would have to land very fast. With a bit of luck, he could lower the undercarriage on the auxiliary system, but it was a once only arrangement working on compressed air and was notoriously unreliable. Once on the ground, he would have no brakes and no nose wheel steering, so he would have to land into the arrestor cable: no problem normally but at high speed potentially dangerous.

Levelling at five thousand feet, he confirmed that the pressure was sufficient in the auxiliary air bottle to lower the undercarriage. He put out an emergency call on the radio to his base. The call was acknowledged at once.

Three minutes later one of the Mirages appeared on his port wing. "Mission zero one, this is Mirage Two Four. You have taken a bird strike on your port mainplane. There is a small amount of damage to the wing undersurface and you are leaking hydraulic fluid. Otherwise OK".

Otherwise OK, thought Sanchar. A chunk of wing torn out, no brakes or flaps and otherwise OK. Only fighter aircrew could find comfort in such a situation. He cursed his stupidity at flying so low over the target. All pilots know that such wrecks are favourite haunts for tired sea birds. "Roger Mirage Two Four, understood. I'm happy to return by myself"

The Mirage acknowledged and broke off in a roar of reheat to the port. The coastline was clearly in view now, and Sanchar set himself for a long, straight-in approach. Holding his breath, he pulled the emergency undercarriage lowering lever. After what seemed an eternity, there were three light bumps as the main and nose wheels locked down. Sanchar breathed again.

"Mission zero one, I now have three greens, gear locked down".

"Roger Zero One. All emergency services have been alerted. The wind is down the runway at fifteen knots".

At ten miles he reduced speed to two hundred knots. The aircraft felt very uncomfortable, and Sanchar realised that the damage to the wing must have been worse than he thought. He dared not reduce speed further for fear of losing control. His mind now crystal clear, his hands steady, he ignored the pounding of his heart and guided the wounded aircraft towards the beckoning runway.

Just as he thought he was home and dry, he realised the aircraft was running out of lateral control, and his inputs from the control column to hold the wings level were becoming progressively less effective. Using full rudder with his right foot, he managed to straighten the wings just in time, but the protesting Super Etendard hit the runway hard and fast in a crabbed attitude. Both tyres burst, mercifully, as a single tyre burst would certainly have slewed him off the runway. He was flung violently forward into his straps as the tailhook hungrily grasped the arrestor cable. As it did so, he closed down the engine to reduce the pressure on the flailing cable. And then all was still and quiet.

The fire vehicle, an ambulance and a car with a very worried-looking Lieutenant Commander Aries arrived as he was scrambling out of the cockpit. He pulled off his heavy helmet and noted that Mantana had also arrived in a screech of tyres. He waited until they were both in front of him. "Gentlemen, you've got some work to do. The pod's not working and the aircraft's a bloody wreck. I want it back on the line by tomorrow afternoon. The firing is going ahead."

CHAPTER 12

Sanchar pulled back the curtain in his office. It was dark outside, and a few wisps of low cloud scudded across the pale autumn moon. On the perimeter track in front of him, two Mirage fighters taxied past on their way to a night interception training mission. Just visible in the dim light of the cockpits, he could make out the vague shapes of the pilots' heads, clad in gaily decorated flying helmets, and bowed forward as they completed their checks before take-off. He had been a pilot for many years, but he could never let an opportunity pass by to watch fighters taking off at night. He knew the thoughts that would be passing through their minds as they prepared to hurl their fragile bodies into the hostile environment of high speed flight. They would be elated, but also a little frightened. Flying complex high performance aircraft called for skill and guts possessed by few men. And at night especially, the workload was as much as one man could absorb. He thought back to the many friends who had momentarily allowed their concentration to slip, and who had paid the ultimate price. With a roar that rattled his windows, the fighters engaged reheat, and in less than a minute the fiery orbs had disappeared amidst the stars in the night sky.

Sanchar sighed and let the curtain fall. He would miss the flying. Whatever the outcome of his mission, he knew that the sortie on May the Second would be his last. Turning back to his maps, he continued to work on the plans that might give him some sort of life for the remainder of his days. He had long since decided that after the attack on the Yacht, his only hope was to make for southern Brazil, eject over land with his aircraft heading out to sea, its autopilot engaged. At low level the land-based radars would not see him, and even allowing for the worst case the aircraft would continue flying for another two hundred miles or more before it ran out of fuel and crashed. Months before, he had identified the Pampas area just north of the Uruguayan border as the best ejection area. During a recent spell of leave, he had driven to the small Brazilian town of Pelotas, just north of Lake Mirius, and had left the car in a garage he had hired for six months. In the boot he had sufficient clothes and personal possessions to see him through. Most importantly, at considerable cost, he had obtained a false Paraguayan passport and driving licence in the name of Fernando Barra. No-one asked too many questions in South America, and he had sufficient confidence in his ability to live on his wits. Yes, even with the unexpected payment to the mysterious caller, he could make another life somewhere. He had calculated precisely the lump sum the Armada would owe him if he were to retire now, and with only a slight twinge of conscience, he had carefully, over the past weeks, been transferring cash from Station resources into his private bank account.

Sanchar was worried about the ejection. Few people survived the experience without some form of injury, normally to the tortured vertebrae of the lower spine. These vulnerable bones are subjected to a force equal to twenty six times the force of gravity as the seat is propelled safely away from the lethal fuselage. And then there was the risk of turning an ankle or, worse, breaking a leg whilst landing on rough terrain. Sanchar tapped his pencil on the maps, and acknowledged philosophically that these were worries peripheral to his principal task, which he had rehearsed to his complete satisfaction. He now just needed the engineers to sort him out a serviceable aircraft, a duty which the humming of generators from the hangar behind his office told him was now in hand.

There was a light knock on the door, and as it half opened, Sanchar saw the smartly uniformed figure of the duty policeman, attending to his routine security checks.

"Oh, I'm sorry, sir," he said, clearly surprised to find his commanding officer working so late into the night.

"It's alright, sergeant," Sanchar reassured him, "I shall be locking up myself and leaving in about half an hour."

"Very good, sir. I'll call back later to double-check your safe."

Sanchar smiled and nodded his approval. The military police had a difficult job and it was good to have them on your side. Carefully, he folded up all his maps and route navigation cards and placed them in a sealed envelope inside a secure container. After locking up, he tore up the several sheets of rough notes that he had been using to confirm the calculations of his final attack profile. It had been a long day and he was looking forward to his customary cognac and then bath before retiring. Taking a last careful look around his office, he switched off the light and walked down the corridor towards the car park.

As the tail lights of his black staff car sped off into the night, the naval policeman appeared out of the shadows, and after checking that no-one was around, he walked quickly into headquarters towards Sanchar's office. Using a small torch only, he checked the desk drawers, confirmed the safe was locked, and finally emptied the torn paper fragments from the waste paper basket into a small plastic bag. As he left, the two Mirages touched down on the runway from their night interception exercise.

∞

"Wake up, sir." Squadron Leader Browne groaned and tried to pull his pillow over his head. "Wake up, sorry, sir," insisted the steward.

Browne reached out and put on the side light. Hunched over him stood the RAF Corporal he had seen in the Mess reception before turning in. "Orderly Officer's on the phone, sir. Signal needing your immediate attention."

"Christ, what time is it?"

"Four thirty, sir. Something about a delay in your trip."

Browne struggled into his flying suit, pulled on the soft, light-brown boots, and after a quick comb of his hair, joined the corporal in the Land Rover.

Five minutes later, they pulled up in a cloud of fine sand outside the operations wing. Browne had long since realised that most people felt they had to drive fast when they had a fighter pilot in the car. He realised it was largely due to some feeling of inferiority, perhaps some need to establish an image that a fighter pilot might respect, but it annoyed him nevertheless.

Inside the whitewashed building he found the equally bleary-eyed Orderly Officer smoking a long American cigarette. Browne nodded and opened the sealed envelope on the desk, marked 'SECRET, FOR THE EYES OF SQUADRON LEADER D BROWNE ONLY'.

The Orderly Officer looked at it inquisitively. "The satellite link has just reported bad weather in the Falklands", he croaked through a plume of cigarette smoke.

"Yes, we're staying here now till Thursday", Browne replied. Ignoring the thinly veiled hint for more information, he folded the signal up, signed for it in the classified register, and wearily stood to go.

"Could you arrange for my crews to be in the main briefing room at eight o'clock please," he asked. "You can tell them the trip's postponed until Thursday and I'll put them in the picture when I see them. I'm going to see if I can get back to sleep."

He couldn't, and by the time he walked into the briefing room, he felt worse than he had three hours before. The crews were obviously in bad humour.

Browne faced up to them with his hands on his hips. "Sorry, gents, but there's a spell of bad weather in the Falklands, and they've just had their first heavy fall of snow at Mount Pleasant airfield. The decision is that we all gather and stay here until Thursday. We'll then fly in pairs at two hour intervals, with a Tristar, to provide top cover over the Yacht from 1200 hours. Providing the weather's picked up, we'll then high tail it to Mount Pleasant. The reserve crews can then take over for a while. Between us we need to keep at least one aircraft on task over the three and a half days that Britannia is in transit from Rio to Montevideo."

The crews groaned in their seats.

"Yes, I know, it's going to be a hell of a slog," he acknowledged.

The grumbling was all part of the macho act, and he knew they would spring to the job when the time came.

"Look on the bright side of life," he went on, "at least you've got time to acquire a nice suntan to show off at home."

"We're going to need a lot of re-planning, sir" said Browne's navigator.

Browne nodded. "Yes, I'm afraid you're right, Mike.

The tanker boys have had a copy of the signal, and they're already working on the route planning. I suggest you get across and join them right away. Let's meet back here at six o'clock local time tonight for an update. In the meantime, be careful not to get too much sun. The cool breeze is very deceptive and I won't take too kindly to anyone who can't strap into his aircraft on Thursday morning. Don't worry; the local girls at Mount Pleasant will still love you."

Flight Lieutenant Curtis took him to one side as the rest wandered off in search of breakfast.

"If we have to come back to Ascension it's going to mean a hell of a long trip, sir." Curtis said in his usual worried manner. "And if we do go on to Mount Pleasant and the weather turns nasty again, the boys are going to be making a tricky approach after over nine hours flying."

"I know, I know, Mike. But it's the only way, and at least we get a few days rest here before we set off. I'll see you later."

As Curtis left, Browne sat down and studied a map of the South Atlantic. They had a lot of ocean to cover, and despite his words, he was more concerned than he had tried to show to his officers.

∞

Turnbull marvelled at the view through the narrow porthole of his cabin. He had spent only two weeks at sea, but had already forgotten the comfort of terra firma, and he thrilled at the striking coastline surrounding Rio de Janeiro. He dressed quickly and joined the Captain on the bridge. The ship had anchored several hundred yards out into the gaily decorated harbour, and several small craft were already bobbing around inquisitively. But the main attraction was undoubtedly the Royal

Yacht, which was already safely berthed against the harbour wall. The Brazilian Navy, however, were very much in evidence, and Turnbull was relieved to see that two grey patrol boats were buzzing around to ensure that other craft kept their distance. On the dockside, he could make out two small armoured vehicles and several police cars in close attendance. The Brazilians were clearly taking every opportunity to avoid any potentially embarrassing incidents.

"Beautiful, isn't it?" Captain Morrison commented, obviously reading Turnbull's thoughts.

"And to think I was feeling homesick for London last night," he joked.

"You can keep it. Give me Rio and Ipanema beach anytime. Are you going to be able to get ashore, Richard?"

Turnbull nodded. "Just for a few hours tonight. I'm going to be busy tomorrow keeping an eye on the Royals' luggage being loaded, and from Tuesday onwards I'm going to be fussing around the Yacht keeping an eye on who's going on and off board. Are you planning a run ashore tonight, David?"

"Don't ask daft questions," the Captain replied wickedly, "And you're welcome to join us if you can keep up."

"I can but try," Turnbull chuckled.

The gentle hum of a helicopter in the distance caught their attention. Squinting into the night sky, Turnbull picked out Cornwall's Lynx threading its way through the tall buildings of the spectacular skyline.

"Is that my visitor?" Turnbull asked.

"Yes. I'm sure you'll want somewhere quiet to talk, so go ahead and use my cabin. You won't be disturbed."

"Thanks, David."

The two men had become good friends during the long voyage down from Southampton, and Turnbull was comforted by the presence of such a steady, reliable confidante at this worrying time. He only wished he could be quite as calm himself.

As the small helicopter settled on the rear deck, Turnbull made his way down to pick up the visitor. He had never met Ralph Prentice before, but he was not surprised at the figure that jumped out of the Lynx to greet him. It seemed to Turnbull that every CIA man wore a light-weight, slightly over-sized suit, with an ill-matching, brightly coloured tie.

He returned the customary exuberant handshake, and guided Prentice away from the rotor blades. "Nice to meet you, Ralph. Let's get off the deck and find somewhere comfortable. I'm sure you're ready for a coffee."

Prentice looked disappointed. "English coffee?" he asked with a hint of a sneer. "I didn't realise the British Navy were dry too."

"The Royal Navy are not dry," Turnbull corrected. "And I promise you that our bad coffee can be made more acceptable with a little sweetener."

"Now you're talking, Richard," Prentice laughed, slapping Turnbull heartily on the back. They found a steward laying out coffee and sandwiches in the Captain's cabin, and after Turnbull had dismissed him they located an unopened bottle of Scotch whisky.

"David Morrison won't mind," Turnbull assured him. "He owes me a few drinks for letting him win at poker just about every night for the last two weeks."

He poured a large measure of the spirit into Prentice's cup and, after some thought, topped up his own coffee. He noticed that Prentice's hands were shaking as he lifted the drink to his lips and drained it in one swallow. Turnbull poured him another large measure; he must have given away his disapproval.

"Yeah, I know it's a bit early," Prentice agreed sheepishly, "But I didn't get too much sleep last night and I need a couple of stiffeners."

"Your business," Turnbull replied non-comittally. "Made any progress?"

"Not much. That bastard Rosario is watching me like a hawk, and I just can't get close to Sanchar. I've got a couple of my men doing some undercover work to see what they can come up with, but they're having to keep a low profile to stay healthy. No British rules here, old chap," Prentice said sarcastically and in an exaggerated public school accent.

Turnbull decided he wasn't going to like this man much. "Haven't you come up with anything at all yet?" he asked irritably.

Prentice picked up the bottle and poured himself another shot of whisky. "Well, we have found out a few things. We know he's a bit of a loner, and he's got no real friends. However, he seems to have a weak spot for girls, and we think he's got some chick in tow in Buenos Aires at the moment. Apparently, he goes down there at least once a week for some physical relief."

Prentice held onto the whisky bottle and settled back in the Captain's leather armchair.

Turnbull wanted to tell him to move out and sit somewhere more appropriate to his semi-inebriated status. But he thought better of it.

"What about the work side?" he asked.

"Not much there either really. They still haven't got their naval air forces sorted out after the Falklands war, and from what our boys can see they don't seem to do much flying at all."

A thought came to Turnbull. "I don't suppose Sanchar still flies himself, does he?"

Prentice pondered for a moment. "I hadn't really thought of that. He's the boss of the base and he's getting on a bit. I guess the only thing he flies is desk."

"Maybe we should check that out a bit more," Turnbull suggested. Prentice saw at once what he was getting at.

"Ah come on, Richard. Even if the guy does still fly, how could he take off from a base in Argentina, get through Brazilian airspace and find one boat amongst thousands that sail around these coasts? It's not like the high seas you know, it'd be like finding a needle in a haystack. And they don't have any weapons worth a dam these days. Come on!"

"Yes, I suppose you're right," Turnbull agreed.

"And anyway, we've got fighter cover for most of the trip down to Montevideo, as well as protection from Cornwall's surface to air missiles. I'm beginning to think that the IRA's refusal to help him plant a bomb was the final straw. He's probably gone and forgotten the whole thing."

"Yeah, that's what I reckon Richard," Prentice slurred. "Shit, there's no way that guy's going to get anywhere near the Queen, so quit worrying will you."

Turnbull nodded, but he couldn't shake off the nagging doubts that he had sown in his own mind.

CHAPTER 13

Inspector Rosario picked a shred of tobacco from his nicotine-stained teeth and flicked it in the general direction of an overflowing waste-paper basket. In front of him several sheets of paper were laid out on the desk, and stuck to each in a crumpled jig-saw arrangement were pieces of paper that had been retrieved from Sanchar's office.

"I can't make any sense of this, my friend," he growled at the passive Sergeant Hugo. "It's just a list of figures, speeds and headings that mean nothing to me at all. Why are you wasting my time?"

Hugo coughed nervously and leaned forward. "Inspector, there are some points of interest which I believe you should know. For a start, the date and time at the top of the first page is the exact moment later this afternoon of the sailing of the Royal Yacht from Rio, and the next figures are the precise time of arrival at Montevideo. These times would be easy to find from any Brazilian newspaper."

Rosario grunted. "What about the rest of the rubbish?" he asked.

"Senor, if you look at this column, it appears to be timings and positions en route. However, you will note that the positions are in fifty mile squares, suggesting that there is an element of uncertainty involved in the calculations."

"And why would that be?" Rosario asked. "Can't the British Navy sail in a straight line?" He laughed in his high, reed-like voice.

"I cannot say for sure, senor, but for security reasons it would seem sensible for the British to keep their route secret, and to ensure that they varied headings on a random basis."

Rosario nodded. Hugo was the only man in his department he completely trusted, and was by far the brightest of his subordinates. He had the evil cunning of a fox, and Rosario respected and even feared him a little for it.

"So what do you make of this, Hugo? Is he planning some form of reception committee at Montevideo, or is he perhaps just an informant for some other organisation?"

"There's not enough to go on here, senor, but we are checking through the rest of the figures on the computer. I've still got two men watching him day and night, and our man at the base is giving us anything that might appear useful."

"But if the British Queen is sailing today, should we not be a bit more worried? I can't pull him in, of course. The Chief of Police would roast me for dinner and feed the scraps to his soldier friends."

Rosario nodded. "I think you are right, senor. He could well be planning some sort of demonstration for the arrival on Saturday. Our informant on the base has advised us that he had booked out overnight this Friday, which would give him time to take the train or drive on Friday evening to Montevideo. Also, Inspector, you will note that there is a time and date heavily underlined here at the bottom of the last page: Four o'clock, Saturday, 2nd May."

∞

Turnbull could have been forgiven for his preoccupation with the safe departure of the Royal Yacht from Rio. However, despite his fears, he could only marvel at the spectacle of their send-off. The visit by Her Majesty had obviously been a resounding success, and it seemed as if the whole of the city had come to cheer themselves hoarse on the harbour walls. As the blue hull of the Yacht slowly slipped away from the quay, a thousand red, white and blue balloons rose into the sky, and a military band struck forth with the Brazilian national anthem. Turnbull should have been concerned at the thousands of craft, large and small that eagerly scurried to escort the Britannia out into the open sea, but there was so much joy in the air that danger seemed far away. Gradually, the Yacht disentangled herself from the slower rowing boats, then the nippy speedboats, and finally from the shiny launches covered with waving Brazilian and British flags. Captain Morrison gave his orders to the young helmsman and the light grey frigate slipped in behind her Mistress.

"I've never seen anything like it before. What a city!" Turnbull exclaimed breathlessly.

"I only wish we could have stayed longer, Richard," Morrison replied. "One night didn't give us nearly enough time to show you Rio properly." They grinned mischievously at each other.

"Did we manage to get everyone back on board?" Turnbull asked.

Morrison sniggered. "Just about. I was a bit worried we might lose you at one stage."

Turnbull nearly blushed. He had indeed let his hair down and drunk too much on Tuesday evening. Still, he reminded himself, he was virtually a single man now, and he felt much more relaxed than he had for months.

"Yes, she was quite a beauty" Richard reminisced. "I wonder if she'll really write to me."

TARGET – THE QUEEN!   *Christopher Coville*

They both laughed and turned their backs on the rapidly disappearing coastline.

∽

As the Royal Yacht slipped her moorings amidst the splendour of Rio de Janeiro, Squadron Leader Des Browne engaged full reheat on his Tornado F3 fighter. Even with the two large external ferry tanks fitted, the aircraft was airborne in less than half the runway's length, as the two Rolls Royce/Turbo Union RB199 engines pushed out over sixteen tons of awesome power. As the undercarriage locked up with a satisfying clunk, the second fighter confirmed that he was safely in the air and was joining up on the port wing. The air was bright and clear, and already Browne could make out the distant white shape of the Tristar tanker that had taken off five minutes earlier. This was going to be the longest sortie Browne had ever flown. It would take three and a half hours just to get to their patrol area some fifty miles out to sea off the Brazilian coast. They would stay on combat patrol for only two hours before handing over to the next pair of fighters. It would then be a very long and tedious transit down to the Falkland Islands. Browne was relieved that the weather at RAF Mount Pleasant had improved, but he was far from complacent. He had served on the Islands many years before, and knew only too well how fickle the weather could be.

"Tanker two miles. We've had permission to join on the tanker's port wing. Ready for pre-joining checks?" Flight Lieutenant Curtis called out from the rear seat.

"Thanks Mike, go ahead."

Curtis went through the long list, making sure the pilot gave the correct responses. All was well.

They both settled down for the long flight, adjusting

their sitting position from time to time as best the small cockpit and ejection seats would allow. Browne smiled as he gazed into the relaxed forward cabin of the Tristar, where the crew were dressed in shirtsleeves and had access to all the luxuries of a large airliner. He often wondered whether the joy and glamour of being a fighter pilot compensated for the discomfort of the occasional long sortie. But despite the ache in his back and the strains on his bladder to come, he knew he could not be satisfied with any other life.

"Five minutes to the first bracket" the tanker captain advised. He sounded nice and relaxed anyway.

Slowly, the long hose with its refuelling basket threaded from under the fat fuselage to trail behind the massive tail. Browne flew his aircraft in behind the gently oscillating hose and carefully guided the refuelling probe into the basket. Fuel flowed from the Tristar into his half-empty tanks. He would refuel just once more on arrival in the patrol area, and then again before departing for the Falklands.

For the next two hours the sky remained a brilliant blue with little cloud below, and when they set up their patrol pattern the coastline of Brazil was clearly visible on the edge of the horizon.

"Nice trip down for the Royals" Curtis noted with a touch of envy.

"Yeah, they'll have the champagne and smoked salmon out by now. Talking about which, I think I'll have a quick bite before we get down to business."

Browne unclipped the lid from the conveniently situated storage box and pulled out a chicken sandwich. "Chicken", he advised his navigator. "Very nice too."

As expected, the next two hours proved uneventful, and Browne again found himself asking why they were being put to so much trouble for no obvious reason. Still, it would be good to see the Falklands again. Despite their remote location, they had a wild beauty all of their own. Like many of his colleagues, he had grown tired of city life, and preferred the solitude of the country, where most operational airfields were sited. Mount Pleasant certainly provided peace and solitude; perhaps too much even for him, he reflected. With a bit of luck he could get out to the coast and see some wild life before his next sortie on Saturday afternoon.

"Contact bearing one-eight zero, low speed, medium level," Curtis called out over the intercom.

Sure enough, on the Foxhunter radar repeater in front of him, a small target return showed on the bright green screen. Rapidly, the computers were going through the process of calculating speed, height and heading.

"Black two from Black one," Browne called to the other fighter, "We have a contact bearing one-eight-zero, going to take a look. Remain on patrol."

"Roger," acknowledged the youthful Flying Officer Kevin Sidwell. Cheekily, his navigator, Flying Officer Pat Thomson asked Browne if he needed any help.

"Negative, stay where you are," Browne ordered over the radio.

"Cheeky young bastards," he chuckled to Curtis as they rolled over and dived down towards the rapidly closing target.

"Range fifteen miles, medium speed, twenty thousand feet, heading north," Curtis droned, his attention glued to the radar console. "It could be the Nimrod .... showing friendly squawk." The electronic identification equipment was showing a friendly return as it interrogated the target aircraft.

"Yes, I can see him now; we'll just pull past and give them a wave."

The Nimrod had left Ascension nearly an hour before

the fighters, and was now descending to set up its anti-submarine patrol pattern, Browne flew his aircraft into close formation on the large grey aircraft's right side, waved to the crewmen who were pressing their faces against the windows, and then pulled up into a steep climbing roll with reheat engaged.

"Let's see them follow that," he said smugly, his body pinned down under the force of gravity.

When they rejoined the Tristar, the next two fighters with their own tanker had already arrived, and after re-filling their tanks, Browne and Sidwell turned their Tornados towards the South. They had been airborne for over six hours and although he still felt fresh, Browne knew that the insidious effects of fatigue would be slowing his reactions and clouding his judgement. He was also a little worried about his young wingman, who was a promising pilot but who had only been on the Squadron for a year. At times like this, it was the steadiness of age and experience rather than the sharpness of youth that mattered. The youngsters always laughed at Browne when he berated them in the bar for their shortage of flying time. More than one had suggested his first log book was written on papyrus, but he remembered the early flying days when he had frightened himself more than most. It had been hard going, with long hours in the bar and the constant pressure to maintain the work-hard, play-hard image. Perhaps he was being too protective. Perhaps every pilot had to go through the same hard school to earn his spurs. But the apprehension wouldn't go away.

"I'll give Mount Pleasant a call on the HF radio and check the weather," Curtis said, rousing Browne from his contemplation.

"Thanks, Mike," he replied, noticing that the cloud

was thickening. Welcome back to the South Atlantic, Browne thought.

Eventually, Curtis managed to make contact with the distant RAF Station - and the news was depressing. Despite the earlier improvement, a sudden spell of snow had temporarily closed the runway for normal operations, and the snow clearance team was frantically working on the landing surfaces. Worse, the wind had picked up from the South, and more snow was forecast.

"Shit," Browne muttered, "That's all we need after this sortie."

Curtis was silent. They had flown together for two years, and both had implicit faith in each other's capabilities. However, this was no ordinary mission, no ordinary destination, and they had shared sufficient perils in the past not to underestimate the task ahead.

One hour later, the news was no better, but by then they had no choice but to continue to the Falklands. Their Tristar had returned to Ascension, and they would be relying upon three other tankers pre-positioned at Mount Pleasant for subsequent sorties. However, from what they heard over the radio, there was no chance of the Commander at Mount Pleasant risking getting a Tristar off the ground in the prevailing weather conditions. Their options were closed.

"Black one to Black two. The runway should be clear by the time we start our approach. I'll go down first and give you a weather check."

"Roger," Sidwell acknowledged. He didn't sound in the least concerned.

As they approached the Falkland Islands, they were picked up on the powerful radar positioned on the top of Mount Kent, the Island's highest mountain. Browne cast off his wingman and after changing to the radar frequency at Mount Pleasant, he descended from twenty thousand feet into the thick, white cloud tops. At once the aircraft was flung around wildly as they entered a vicious snow-storm. Fighting to maintain control, Browne levelled off at two thousand feet, lowered his flaps and undercarriage and slowed to approach speed.

"Christ, Mike, this is going to be a tricky one. Give me a shout as we pass two hundred feet, and let me know if you see anything on the ground," Browne asked.

The radio burst into life. "Black one, this is Mount Pleasant Talkdown. Turn starboard zero nine degrees and descend to fifteen hundred feet. You have two miles to run to the glidepath."

Browne acknowledged. "Roger, check present weather."

"Mount Pleasant is red in snow, with full cloud cover at one hundred feet. The runway is open, but breaking action is poor. One mile to glidepath."

Browne swallowed hard and began the slow descent towards the runway threshold. The air was turbulent and the windscreen blow system was barely coping with the swirling snow. Trying to put his fatigue to one side, he fought to fly as accurately as he could.

"You are on the glidepath, one mile to touchdown. Take over visually."

"Two hundred feet," Curtis called out.

Browne looked out through the head-up display; nothing but snow and whiteness. He got another warning shout from Curtis as they passed one hundred feet, and was just pushing the throttles forward to overshoot when, miraculously, the snow briefly cleared, and the bright approach lights suddenly came into view. Browne chopped back the throttles, banked violently, and slammed the aircraft down heavily onto the glistening surface. The Tornado slewed to one side as reverse thrust bit, and it took all of Browne's years of experience to stop the aircraft from leaving the runway. Gradually, he brought it under control, disengaged reverse thrust, and taxied clear onto the snow-packed perimeter track.

"You can start breathing again now," he said shakily.

"That was a bit nasty," Curtis remarked.

Understatement was in order on such occasions, but Curtis's heart was still pounding furiously. He gradually unwound, and looked around at the barren Falklands landscape. It was hard to believe that these strange Islands represented so much in recent British history. He shook himself back to reality as they headed towards the operations area.

A heavily clad team of groundcrew ushered them into dispersal. As Browne was closing down, they heard the roar of jet engines behind them as the other Tornado overshot in the thick cloud.

"Christ, Kevin didn't get in. Let's get up to the tower quickly."

A very worried Wing Commander was waiting in his Land Rover. He was the senior operations officer, and after a brief welcome they swept off towards Air Traffic Control. Inside, they found the Station Commander, Group Captain Boz Panton, and another senior officer Browne didn't recognise.

Browne smiled at his old friend. "Hello, sir, good to see you again."

"Not much of a welcome, Des," Panton said grimly. "You looked as though you only just made it. This is Group Captain Tony Merton from MOD."

Browne nodded. "What's the position with our aircraft, sir?" he asked anxiously.

"Well, we've managed to get the message to the others to return to Ascension. This weather should be through in a few hours and it looks OK for the next few days. Black two is downwind for another radar approach. He couldn't see anything last time."

"I'm not surprised. We were bloody lucky," Browne admitted. "How much fuel has he got left?"

"He says he can make another four approaches, and then ..."

They all knew that ejection in these conditions would be fatal. A young corporal handed them both large mugs of steaming coffee.

"Thanks, corporal." Curtis said appreciatively. "We don't half need this."

Browne sat down and watched helplessly. If anything, the weather was getting worse, and the snow clearance teams were desperately using the available minutes to try and clear the touchdown area. As Black two approached five miles from the airfield, the vehicles were ordered off the runway. In the background, the talk-down controller continued his steady monologue, guiding the Tornado skilfully in height and heading towards the landing point.

When the blip on the radar disappeared off the bottom of the cathode ray display, the controller handed over the final stage of the landing to the pilot. "Take over visually."

All eyes in the control tower turned towards the end of the runway, still obscured by driving snow. Suddenly there was a blinding flash ... the whiteness became tinged with orange, and in grotesque slow motion, the Tornado appeared, bouncing ... cartwheeling ... wrapped in flames. Fists clenched ... eyes stared unbelievingly ... before the mouths could scream it collided with a parked snow clearance vehicle and exploded in a ball of oily black smoke and fire. For a few seconds, everyone was stunned.

The Commanding Officer grabbed Browne by the arm. "Come on, let's get down there."

In a daze, Browne stumbled downstairs and flung

himself into the Station Commander's Land Rover as it started to speed across the tarmac towards the wreckage, which was already surrounded by fire engines.

As they arrived, the fire chief came running up to them. "We've just picked up the Navigator. He ejected just as the aircraft was hitting the ground. OK - just a broken leg," he panted. "The two men in the snow vehicle are both badly burned ... I don't think they'll make it!"

"What about the pilot?" Browne screamed over the noise of the sirens.

The fire chief shook his head, and turned to look at the remains of the barely recognisable Tornado which was still smouldering, parts of its blackened fuselage jutting out through the layers of foam.

The South Atlantic had claimed another victim.

∞

It's your Squadron Commander from UK, sir," the ops assistant said, handing Browne the secure telephone.

"Hello, sir, Des here."

"Hi, Des. Christ, we're all shattered here about young Kevin Sidwell. Any chance at all he might have got out?"

"No, I'm afraid not, sir. They've just pulled his body from the wreckage. Pat Thomson managed to eject ... broken leg. He'll be alright. Two snow clearance operators were badly burned ... one's already dead."

"OK, Des. I'll let Kevin's family know." He paused for a minute.

"Des, I know you won't feel much like talking about the mission now ..."

"I'm OK, sir. We can manage from tomorrow when I get the other aircraft in, but I could do with another crew on tomorrow's Tristar."

"Yeah, leave that to us Des. I'm sorry to have put it

this way, but the MOD's been on to the CO here, and they're adamant that you're to pick up the task as soon as possible. What's the weather doing now?"

"The snow belt has gone through and it's looking a lot more settled. I've just spoken to the met man and he says it should be fine until Sunday at least."

They signed off. Des felt sorry for his boss; it was a lousy job having to tell a mother and father that their young boy was dead. Well, Browne thought bitterly, at least the Royal Yacht should have a pleasant few days cruising.

CHAPTER 14

Sanchar turned the shower to full and gritted his teeth as the pulsing jets of cold water attacked and invigorated his naked body. He felt good. The sortie had gone well, the jamming pod was working to perfection, and the Exocet attack profile had been a resounding success. Even Lieutenant Colonel Aries had smiled when he got a thumbs up from Sanchar as he was taxying on to the ramp. And the weather for the next day was good enough, with layered cloud above three thousand feet and some isolated thunderstorms further south. That would suit his plans very well indeed; the layered cloud would provide concealment should he need it, and the electrical atmospheric activity would cause communication and radar problems for any other aircraft airborne.

His flesh tingling and his mind crystal clear, he vigorously towelled himself down and changed into uniform. It was nearly eleven o'clock. He had arranged to visit his local bank at noon, and then he would head off to Buenos Aires for a last night with Sabina. He hadn't seen her for weeks, and he yearned for the comfort that her body would bring. He knew, also, that he needed the distraction and satisfaction of their sexual union to ensure a peaceful night.

Sanchar found Aries and Commander Mantana waiting in his office. "Excellent, gentlemen," he said, slapping Aries heartily on the back. "My congratulations to your men, Aries. They have had to work hard,

I know, but the aircraft was in superb shape today. You'll pass on my thanks?"

Aries nodded. "Of course, sir. I expect to have both aircraft ready for tomorrow. Are you still going for a three o'clock take-off time?"

"Yes. The weather forecast looks good. What about the Mirages?"

"No problem, sir." Mantana replied. "We have plenty of serviceable aircraft, and there will still be a reserve in hand, manned up and ready to go if you need it. But I'm sure you won't."

Sanchar was satisfied. He opened his desk drawer and brought out a bottle of cognac and poured three generous measures. "Salud, my friends. Here's to a successful firing."

They joined him in the toast, not realising that they were raising their glasses to the success of the greatest crime of the Century.

∞

Although he was entitled to twenty four hours off duty after his long sortie the day before, Browne hadn't been able to relax. The image of the blazing tomb of Kevin Sidwell's Tornado had haunted his brief period of sleep, and he felt too caught up with the whole operation to leave the decision making to someone else. The remaining aircraft had been arriving at two hourly intervals during the day, and the reserve crews, fresh and eager, had been pacing around whilst the groundcrew toiled to refuel the aircraft in good time for the next sortie. The replacement pilot and navigator would be arriving that night, and he was happy to fly them on the mid-morning wave, which would cover the period from noon to three o'clock over the Yacht. He and Mike Curtis would take over from them until five o'clock.

TARGET – THE QUEEN! *Christopher Coville*

That, thank God, he thought, would be the end of their commitment. They would then be able to get a couple of days rest before flying the aircraft back on the Tuesday. He would be glad to get home, but he dreaded the funeral that had been scheduled for the Friday morning. There was something particularly heart-rending about a service funeral, and experience of bidding a last farewell to so many friends in the past left him in no doubt that it would be painful. But it had to be done properly; that much they owed to their colleague and his family.

Browne was a loyal officer, and despite the accident he had managed to keep a brave face and sustain the professionalism and morale of his men. But he was still wondering whether it was all worth the heavy risk, not to mention the price already paid, to provide such a token gesture. Surely it was all an over-reaction from the top brass? He shook his head grimly and headed for the Mess.

As always, Sanchar left his car parked in a garage a discreet distance away from Sabina's home. With nearly twenty thousand US dollars in the boot, he was particularly careful to ensure the doors were locked firmly and the garage secure. He smiled to himself. His fussy, bespectacled bank manager had tried hard to maintain a proper professional manner, but he had obviously been bursting to ask a lot of questions. Sanchar had partially satisfied the man's curiosity by suggesting, with a sly wink, that he had a secure investment in hand, and would be returning the cash and more in a few months. But for the second time in a week, he had left the man more than a little bemused as he stuffed the banknotes into a brown leather satchel before bidding him farewell.

It was a cool bright day in Buenos Aires. Sanchar was casually, but neatly dressed: well enough to be welcomed at any good restaurant, but not so formal as to arouse too much interest. He strolled up the street towards Rosita's fruit shop. As usual, she was chattering happily with a cluster of other women. He rarely saw anyone buying anything at her shop, but there always seemed to be a host of customers jostling around the fruit stalls. The group became quiet as he approached, and a couple of women drifted away. The rest turned their faces and tried to hide their smiles. Feeling a little self-conscious, Sanchar greeted Rosita, and gave her a small box of sweets. He knew she liked to be remembered in these little ways. She kissed him gently on both cheeks, and pointed upwards.

Sabina was waiting for him in her darkened bedroom. She was naked, save for a thick leather belt round her waist and a white silk scarf around her brown shoulders. Sanchar tried to say her name, but his voice seized in his throat. He rushed into her arms without anything said, fell on the bed and took her frantically and hungrily.

Sabina nudged him again. "Wake up, darling, it's nearly seven o'clock."

Sanchar stirred from the best sleep he'd had for weeks and looked up at her face. She looked happy, contented. He kissed her gratefully, and with a bull-like roar heaved himself out of bed. "I've booked a table for eight. We'd better get a move on. I'm going to buy you the best dinner you've ever had in your life."

She giggled excitedly and led him through to the shower. Together they stood under the cool water, enjoying the feel of each other's wet skin. Sanchar slapped her wet rump with relish. "Come on, we'll never get out at this rate," he chuckled.

In a few minutes they were tumbling downstairs, their hair still glistening wet. Rosita waved them goodbye, and watched as they disappeared up the hill. She shook her head sadly, and wondered how long it would be before her pretty daughter's heart would be broken by this strange man. She was worrying as mothers do the world over, when a hand on her shoulder made her jump.

"Senora, we should like to talk with you please."

There were two men. One, short and built like an ox, held her firmly. She shuddered as he pushed a dreaded police identification card in her face.

"I have done nothing, nothing," she protested.

They smiled. She was frightened, and for them that was a good start. "Don't worry, senora, we only want a little chat with you. Inside please."

Rosita was forced into the front room and pushed roughly into her old armchair. She started to get hysterical as they knelt down in front of her. The second man, pockmarked and heavily-jowled, slapped her sharply across the face. Sobbing jerkily, she slowly got herself under control.

The ugly one put a forefinger firmly on the tip of her nose. "That's better, senora. Now, we just want to talk to you about your daughter's sailor boy." He smiled, but with menace in his face.

Rosita recoiled at the odour of his breath as he came closer. "I don't know anything," she stammered hoarsely.

"Where are they going tonight, senora?" the short man asked quietly.

"To some night club in town. I don't know which one."

He raised his fist.

She cried out in fear. "I swear I don't know."

"And when will they come back?"

"I don't know. I swear I don't know. My daughter,

Sabina, she took a small bag. Perhaps they are staying somewhere tonight. They didn't tell me," she pleaded.

The pock faced man swore. They had not anticipated Sanchar staying overnight. He stroked Rosita's face. Her eyes were wide with fear.

"Alright, senora," he purred. "Now just settle down and tell us everything you know about Captain Sanchar."

The knocking on the door woke Sanchar. He looked around the hotel room. Sabina lay half covered by the single silky sheet. The rest of the room looked as though twenty people had enjoyed a riotous party. Strewn around the floor were half empty champagne bottles, and discarded oyster shells. On the bedside table lumps of caviar and pieces of lemon floated on melted ice. The knock on the door sounded again.

"OK, OK. One minute please."

He wrapped a towel round his waist, tidied up the worst of the mess, and rather sheepishly opened the door. The waitress pretended not to see the shambles as she pushed the heavily laden breakfast trolley into the room. Sanchar bought her silence with a generous tip, and promised to leave more for the cleaning staff. She seemed happy with the arrangement.

Sabina stirred with a frown as Sanchar turned on the shower. "Quick! Turn off that noise.....Oh, my head."

He laughed and threw a wet sponge across the room at her back. She shrieked and threw it back in mock rage.

Neither of them felt much like food after the excesses of the previous night, but experience had long ago taught Sanchar the therapeutic effects of a healthy breakfast. They ate in silence as the memories of the night before came tumbling back.

"What a night, darling," she sighed reaching across for his hand.

Sanchar smiled, looked at his watch and jumped up to dress quickly. Sabina stretched out like a cat on the bed, and watched him with interest. He combed his hair carefully, and after checking in the mirror, took her in his arms.

She held him tightly. "Darling, those things you were saying last night. You frightened me. Who is Alfredo and what....?"

Sanchar put a finger gently on her lips. "Don't take any notice of me. I'd had far too much champagne."

She was still uneasy, but she shrugged her shoulders resignedly, and put her head against his shoulder.

"I have to go now," he said, softly kissing her forehead. "I'm flying this afternoon and I need to be back by noon. There's something in an envelope on the table for your taxi. I'll settle the hotel bill, but you stay on for a few hours if you want."

He kissed her goodbye, wiped the tears from her cheeks, and left. He didn't look back. Somehow she knew she would never see him again.

"I've just heard from Prentice," Turnbull said to Morrison. "I can't stand that greasy little bastard, but I suppose I'm going to have to learn to be nice to him."

"Anything happening?" Captain Morrison asked.

"Apparently Sanchar left his base for Buenos Aires as it seems he does most Fridays. He didn't appear to be carrying more than a weekend's worth of luggage, and he kept a date with his girlfriend. Prentice says they spent the night in a hotel somewhere on the coast, and they were still shacked up there at nine o'clock this morning. He's pretty sure they're planning to stay there all weekend."

"I don't blame him," Morrison added wryly. "These bloody fighter pilots always seem to get the best girls, while we do all the hard graft out here at sea."

Turnbull laughed and turned to look at the Royal Yacht rising and falling gently into the light swell. She looked magnificent, despite her long journey from the South of England, and he could hardly believe that anything could seriously threaten her.

The intercom buzzed from the operations room. "Mission Five-Four Alpha is just handing over to Five-Four Bravo, sir. Is it OK if he does a low pass?"

"Delighted," Morrison replied. "Confirm all weapons safe?"

There was a slight pause. "All weapons safe, sir. He'll be across in three minutes from the North."

Turnbull and Morrison walked outside to the rear of the superstructure and searched across the bow into the distant sky.

"There he is," Morrison exclaimed, his better trained eyes catching sight of a glint of metal in the distance. A small puff of smoke appeared as the pilot of the Tornado selected reheat. With wings swept fully back, the sleek grey aircraft streaked noiselessly across the top of the frigate, a frightening roar arriving a second later. As its speed approached the sound barrier, a shock wave shimmered across the fuselage. With wing tips trailing vortices, it smoothly pulled up to the vertical, gradually growing smaller and smaller, until suddenly it burst into contrails five miles above in the dark blue sky.

Turnbull turned to Morrison, his ears still ringing. "You know, David, I think I can see why they always get the prettiest girls!"

TARGET – THE QUEEN! *Christopher Coville*

As they strolled back for a coffee on the bridge, one of the prettiest girls in Buenos Aires was about to be pitched into a bloody and terrifying nightmare.

CHAPTER 15

Sabina sang cheerfully to herself as she tidied up her hair and put the finishing touches to her make-up. She had good reason to be happy, now the better for one thousand US dollars she had found in the envelope with her taxi fare. Sanchar had obviously paid her off, but although she was very fond of him, his strange ways had always frightened her a little. And there were other men around who would happily snap her up in return for her favours. No, it was perhaps for the best that he had decided to call it a day. She would have to break the news gently to her avaricious mother, but a crispy hundred dollar bill should help ease her grief at their parting.

With scarcely a backward glance at their last meeting place, Sabina slammed the door closed and headed for the reception desk. A spotty, shy young man in a black suit self-consciously ordered her a taxi, his eyes only lifting from the desk as she turned to leave. As she tripped out into the sunlight, a large white Mercedes drew up in front of the hotel, and the unctuous driver swept her into the deep, leather-clad rear seat. This was the way she liked to live, driven by an attentive chauffeur in a large limousine, with all heads turning as she passed.

The neighbours would be green with envy, she reflected smugly. She didn't care a fig what they would say about how she came to be driven back home at one o'clock in the afternoon in a white Mercedes. Most of the pompous old men who scolded her would do anything to get into her bed, and their women knew it only too well.

She stopped at the bank to deposit eight hundred dollars in her account. Hopefully, her mother would believe that Sanchar had left her only two hundred dollars and would be content with an equal split. And why not, Sabina thought. Her mother didn't have to thrash around underneath him all night to get her slice of the cake.

Sabina was surprised not to find Rosita in front of her shop as she normally was on a Saturday afternoon. Looking around the street, she noticed that it was deserted, and several of the windows had curtains drawn. As she got out of the car, she saw the face of the old lady next door appear briefly at the window before jumping back like a frightened squirrel.

A wave of fear washed over Sabina turning her legs to jelly. Had something happened to her mother, she wondered. Quickly paying the driver, all thoughts of making the neighbours envious gone, she practically ran through the shop into the small living room. Her mother was sitting in the old armchair. Her face was rigid with fear, and blood oozed from her swollen mouth and nose. She seemed to be totally oblivious to her daughter's return home. Sabina cried out and was rushing towards Rosita when hands grabbed her and held her tightly. She gasped, then yelled out in pain as both her arms were mercilessly wrenched back, forcing her head down between her knees. Viciously kicking her legs from under her, a man leapt onto her chest and forced the cold steel of a gun barrel between her teeth. She gagged as the sharp metal hit the back of her mouth.

"I'm just about to blow your brains all over your Mama's nice carpet, you little whore," the man snarled, his rank breath warm on her perspiring forehead.

She closed her eyes, waiting for the explosion she

knew would end her life. Slowly the barrel was drawn from between her lips, and sobbing in terror she opened her eyes.

The man lowered the gun and put it against her throat. "Where is Sanchar?" he demanded.

Sabina tried to speak, but her voice came out in a strangled croak. The man forced the gun into the soft flesh of her neck.

She whimpered and forced out a few words in desperation. "He's....he's gone back to base,....he's gone back to Puerto Belgrano."

"You lying little bitch," the man shouted, hitting the side of her face with his left hand. "Where is he? If you lie again I'll blow your throat to bits."

"I swear it. I swear it. He's gone back to fly."

The man cursed and stood up. The gun was shaking in his hand. "OK, let's get her down to the station. And you, you bitch, keep your mouth closed or we'll come back and finish you off properly."

Rosita remained frozen, her eyes wide in terror, as the two policemen dragged Sabina out through the back door and threw her into a waiting car.

༺༻

Prentice couldn't believe his ears.

"What d'you mean, he's gone back to the Base? Shit, Reilly, you told me he'd booked out for the weekend. Yeah, OK, you call me back as soon as you can. I'm going to start drafting an Immediate signal to Turnbull, but you make damned sure you call me back within fifteen minutes."

His secretary came scurrying in as Prentice bellowed through the open door. "Martha, get me a signal pad quick - and tell the comms centre to get ready for a top priority signal in clear. I haven't got time for code."

Cursing, he checked his watch. It was nearly half past one. He scribbled out the opening lines of the signal:

TO HMS CORNWALL
IMMEDIATE/TOP PRIORITY/ CONFIDENTIAL STOP PERSONAL FOR TURNBULL FROM PRENTICE STOP SUBJECT HAS UNEXPECTEDLY RETURNED TO BASE....

He stopped and waited, watching the telephone. It seemed an eternity before it rang. Frantically he picked it up.

"Prentice," he announced breathlessly, his chest heaving. "Yeah, Reilly, Christ Almighty! Are you sure? Right, stay exactly where you are. What's the number you're on? OK. Now stay there, Reilly, and don't let anyone else use that fucking phone."

He slammed the receiver down, shouted for his secretary, and with trembling hands completed the signal:

BASE IS BEING BROUGHT TO OPERATIONAL STATUS STOP TWO SUPER ETENDARDS AND THREE MIRAGES ARE BEING TOWED OUT OF THEIR HANGARS STOP FLYING ACTIVITY SEEMS IMMINENT STOP.

"Martha, get that off right now....I mean right now. And get the Ambassador on the phone. I don't give a shit where he is, I've gotta talk to him now. It's an emergency."

∞

It was just after two fifteen when Turnbull received the ominous signal from Prentice. He and Morrison reread the curt message, and then stared at each other in disbelief.

"Are they really planning something, Richard?"

Morrison asked in amazement.

"I just don't know, David. They don't normally fly on a Saturday, and the fact that Sanchar himself has gone back smells very nasty to me. I don't think we can take any chances."

Morrison nodded. "You're right. The Tornados are just about to change over, so at least we'll have a fresh crew on patrol. Looking at the timescale, I'll go to full action stations at three o'clock. I'd better have a word with the Admiral of the Yacht and put him in the picture."

"Can we get more aircraft to give top cover?" Turnbull asked.

"I can try. We could keep the aircraft that's on patrol now for a bit longer, I suppose. I'll get a signal off to Mount Pleasant. Is there anything else we can do on the mainland?"

"I'd better have a word with London. If we get any further signs that something's up, London may want to consider asking the Brazilians to help. I suppose they could start shouting at the Argentineans themselves."

Turnbull scratched his head. "I wonder if this is something official or if it's just Sanchar doing his own thing."

"Well he couldn't have picked a better day," Morrison said.

"What do you mean?" Turnbull queried, turning to look at the Captain.

"Have you forgotten? For crying out loud, Richard, it's May the Second, the anniversary of the sinking of the Belgrano!"

∞

Sergeant Hugo knocked softly and peered around the door at Rosario. "She is ready for you now, Inspector."

Rosario nodded and stubbed out his cigar in the overflowing ashtray. "Usual place?"

"Yes, senor. No-one else knows."

Many years before, Rosario had found the perfect den for his interrogations, well away from the eyes of his superiors. A cousin of Hugo's who was the solitary policeman on a border crossing into Uruguay, would turn a blind eye to activities in his cell for a small cost, which Rosario took out of police accounts. No-one had ever noticed.

"Is she saying anything?" Rosario asked.

"The boys are, shall we say, softening her up," Hugo sniggered. "I don't think she will cause any problems for you."

Thirty minutes later, they drew up outside the plain concrete building, which stood alongside a lonely dirt-track barred by a rusty metal pole. The only sound was from the large sea birds circling overhead.

"They want their lunch, eh Inspector," Hugo said pointing to the sky.

They both laughed.

"Let us not disappoint them, my friend," Rosario replied.

Inside the dark cell, Sabina was suspended from a wooden beam, her wrists tied together with wire, and her toes just touching the damp stone floor. She bore the unmistakeable marks of rape; her once beautiful face was now black and swollen. Behind her, sitting on a wooden table, the two young policemen drank beer in gulps from large brown bottles. With them was Hugo's cousin, a fat, swarthy man with a fleshy face. He was puffing furiously and had scratch marks on his neck and forehead.

Rosario greeted him affectionately. "My dear Sergeant Benitez. As always it is a pleasure to see you again. You look as if you have been taking a little exercise."

Benitez snorted. "She's a wildcat, that one Inspector. But she's a little more tame now, I think."

Rosario laughed and slapped him on the back. "You want to be careful at your age, my friend. You're not a young buck any more you know."

"You wouldn't say that if you'd been here ten minutes ago, senor," one of the policemen said between gulps of beer. They laughed raucously.

Rosario turned towards Sabina and slowly took off his jacket. She whimpered as he came close to her face, first smiling and then snarling as his nose touched hers. Shouting as loudly as he could, his spit spraying onto her mouth and chin, he asked her name.

Sabina was terrified. "Sabina Calvez," she whispered.

"I didn't hear you," Rosario shouted.

"Sabina...Sabina Calvez," she said again desperately trying to raise her voice.

"That's better, Sabina. Now that we know who you are, I want you to tell me where you were last night, and who you were with."

Rosario nodded again, and one of the policemen released the pressure on the wire, allowing Sabina's feet to settle on the floor. She staggered, but was held upright by another tug from the gloating assistant.

"Now don't go falling over when you are talking to the Inspector," Hugo shouted. He could barely conceal his growing excitement.

"I was with Captain Sanchar," she croaked, "in a hotel by the River."

"Good," Rosario said, feigning pleasure. "Good girl, you are doing very well. Bring the young lady a chair. We must look after our pretty young guest better."

Sabina was pushed down onto a rough wooden stool. Hugo stood behind her, and when her head fell forward as she fainted he pulled back viciously on her hair.

"Look at the Inspector when he is talking to you, Sabina."

TARGET – THE QUEEN!   *Christopher Coville*

"Good, good," crooned Rosario. He pulled up a stool himself, sat down a few feet away from Sabina, and slowly lit himself a cigar.

He waited for a while, blowing smoke into her face. "Now Sabina, we don't want to hurt you."

One of the men stifled a laugh.

"But we must have some information which I think you have. Now where has Captain Sanchar gone this afternoon?"

Sabina sobbed quietly. "He said he was going back.... back to the Base.... to fly I think."

"You think, Sabina, you think." Leaning forward he screamed back at her, "Don't think - tell me where he has gone and why."

"He has gone to the base to fly," she replied, her bloodshot eyes pleading.

"Now, my girl. What is Captain Sanchar doing when he flies? He must have told you something while he was with you all last night."

Sabina shook her head. "I don't know any more..... please believe me, Inspector. I don't understand what he does at the Base."

Rosario shrugged his shoulders, stood up and left the cell. Outside, he was joined by Hugo's cousin, who handed him a bottle of beer.

Rosario took in a deep breath of air. "You need to clean your prison better, Sergeant Benitez. It's starting to smell of too many previous clients."

They both laughed as in the background Sabina's screams came up from the underground cell.

"How is your dear wife, Sergeant?" Rosario asked, ignoring the noises from inside.

"Well, thank you, Inspector. But she is now getting a little old and is better in the kitchen than in the bed."

"Never mind, my friend. I'm sure today will do you

good. She's quite a beauty, eh?"

Benitez cackled and rubbed his neck. "Yes, senor, but how do I explain these scratches to my wife tonight?"

"Tell her you fell into a bed of thickets my friend."

They both laughed and drank from their bottles.

Hugo came out and nodded to Rosario.

"Ah, good. Come on in, my dear Sergeant Benitez. I don't think we shall be keeping you very much longer."

Sabina was again suspended from the beam, but now her legs were spread apart and her feet tied down to metal rings on the floor. Two large coils of wire were connected to her body.

"All wired up, I see Sabina," Rosario exclaimed in mock surprise. "Now let's try again. I want you to tell me anything you know about Captain Sanchar's movements this afternoon."

Sabina shook her head. "I do not know any more, senor."

At once her body went into a frantic spasm as Hugo switched on the electric current. Like a grotesque rag doll, her head was flung back, and her tongue was thrust out obscenely. As quickly, she slumped back as the current was switched off. Rosario waited for a minute as she choked and vomited onto the floor.

"Now Sabina, that was two seconds. The next time it will be five seconds and then ten. You will not die until we get up to one minute, and that will be a long way away yet. So......let's try again shall we. I cannot believe that Captain Sanchar has known you all this time and has told you nothing of his plans. I will ask you once more, my lovely one, what type of flying is he doing today?"

Sabina shook in fear, and sobbed in despair. "I....I don't know. He never tells me about his job.....there's only the dreams and....and when he is upset."

Rosario leapt forward. "What dreams, what dreams?

What has he said?"

He nodded to Hugo and her body jerked backwards in spasm once more. After five seconds she collapsed onto the wire, her eyes pits of blood and her chest heaving. Rosario moved backwards in disgust as her bowels opened onto the wet floor.

"Clean up this filth, Sergeant Benitez," he called out.

Benitez brought out a hose pipe and sluiced the mess into a gutter which led to a gaping drain. When he had finished he turned the icy water over Sabina, keeping the jet on her face. She choked as the water clogged her throat and nostrils.

"Good. Thank you Sergeant. Now Sabina, tell me exactly what he said in his dreams."

She could scarcely speak, and Rosario had to move forward as her swollen lips moved slowly. "He kept saying a name....Alf....Alfredo."

Rosario pulled her head up. "And what else did he say? What else?"

"Wanted to get back....at the British....didn't make sense."

Rosario swore. She was drifting in and out of consciousness. He slapped her face as hard as he could and pulled her chin up.

"Come on, he must have said more. How was he going to get even with the British? Tell me, tell me," he shrieked.

"Didn't make sense....sinking Britain.....attacking Britain....the Queen."

"How was he going to sink Britain, you little fool? What do you mean?"

"Don't know, just sinking Britain....the Queen."

Suddenly Rosario realised what she was saying. "Mother of Christ. Did he say Britain...or did he say Britannia. - Royal Yacht Britannia?"

Sabina nodded feebly. "Yes...yes...yacht....Britannia."

Rosario flung her head to one side and called Hugo outside. "Hugo, this could be very dangerous. I think the mad fool must be planning to attack the British Royal Yacht this afternoon. We must get to the Base at once."

As they raced to Hugo's car, one of the policemen called out to them. "What about the girl, senor?"

Rosario looked up at the sky as the car started up. "The birds look very hungry....do you have anything nice for their lunch?"

The policeman laughed as the silver Mercedes sped off in a cloud of dust and stones. It was nearly two o'clock.

CHAPTER 16

Every nerve in Sanchar's body was tingling. He had never felt so alive as he walked into the Briefing Room. Mantana and Aries followed him and sat down as the Meteorological officer switched on the overhead projector.

"Good afternoon Captain," he started, clicking his heels together.

Sanchar nodded.

"The cold front that gave us the sleet and rain yesterday has now passed through and we are in an unstable westerly flow."

He changed slides to show a cross section of the afternoon's weather. "As you can see, sir, there should be no problem with cloud or visibility, with five eighths cover at three thousand feet, and virtually nothing above. The wind will be westerly, ten to fifteen knots with occasional gusts up to twenty."

"What about the Malvinas?" Sanchar asked.

"They have had some heavy snowstorms over the past few days, sir, but they are now in a similar weather pattern to ourselves. Their only problem is going to be the occasional thunderstorm to the north of the Islands."

"OK, thanks. Engineering briefing please."

Aries stood up and addressed the group. "No problems, Captain. We have two Super Etendards and three Mirages on the line, and another Etendard is ready in the hangar if you need it. But the primary aircraft are in great shape", he added confidently.

"I hope you're right," Sanchar said dryly. "Thank you. Anything on the Ops side?"

Mantana stood up. "The RAF is busier than usual on the Malvinas, sir. They did fly one fighter sortie this morning, but it could have been just an air test."

Sanchar stopped him. "What about those Tornado F3s that deployed to Ascension? Do we have any further information on what they're up to?"

"No, sir," Mantana replied. "I've spoken to the intelligence boys and they think they're still there."

Sanchar sucked the end of his chinagraph pencil. "That seems a bit strange to me," he said. "I find it difficult to believe that the British would deploy their newest fighter to the middle of the Atlantic for no good reason."

"It could be connected to the visit by the British Queen to Brazil," Mantana suggested. "There's something in this morning's papers about it."

"I can't see what good they'd be doing at Ascension," Sanchar muttered. "OK, let's get on with the tactics brief."

The Mirage flight commander spoke for a few minutes about his interceptions, and Sanchar paid particular attention to the briefing by Mantana on the Exocet Trial profile.

"If I may just remind you, sir," he concluded, "to be very careful after you fire the missile. Remember you have the problem of a heavy fuel tank on the other wing, which would give you noticeable imbalance once the missile has gone. If you still have any fuel in it after firing, you will have an uncomfortable ride home. If you don't like the way the aircraft is flying, just get rid of the rank over the sea before making your final approach."

Sanchar stood up. "Thank you, gentlemen. You've all put a lot of work into this trial, and I delighted that you've managed to meet my deadline for today. Please pass on my thanks to all your people. Could I just remind you of the need for total security. There is to be no response to any enquiry from outside, from whatever source. We don't often fly on Saturdays, so we can expect some interest from the police or the media. I have already instructed our security police to be extra vigilant and to deny access to anyone who does not have a valid reason for entering the Base."

The operations officer stood up and gave a final time check. It was two thirty.

∽

Squadron Leader Browne cursed to himself. It had been unavoidable, but perhaps he could have been smarter. The large thunder cloud had been concealed by the thin sheet of stratocumulus at three thousand feet, and as he came climbing clear of the lower layer he had been confronted by its massive blackness immediately in their path. The aircraft lurched as a flash of lightning lit up the sky.

"Did we pick up that lightning strike, Mike?" he asked anxiously. The ensuing clap of thunder had certainly seemed close.

"I don't think so, sir," Curtis replied. "The radar did flash a couple of times but it seems OK now."

Browne thought for a moment. "Righto, Mike. Let's keep going, but if we have any more trouble, we'd better get back to Mount Pleasant. How long before we arrive at the patrol area?"

"We'll be there in about forty five minutes. I'll just see if I can raise Cornwall on the HF radio and let them know we're on the way."

For the first two or three minutes, Curtis was unable to raise the ship on the radio, but eventually the background interference faded and the radio officer on board HMS Cornwall replied to their call.

"Roger, Mission Black Zero, Three. Stand by for urgent message. Possible attack on Group within next few hours. Mission Black Zero Two is remaining on patrol with you until fifteen thirty hours. We have requested further aircraft, estimate on task sixteen thirty hours. Will advise further when information available."

Browne acknowledged. "Ye Gods," he exclaimed breathlessly. "What the hell's going on?"

"Surely it can't be the Argies?" Curtis said in disbelief.

They were both silent for a moment, as the enormity of the message sank in. Just then the radar flashed and switched itself off.

"Shit! The bloody radar's just tripped off." Curtis exclaimed. "That lightning strike's obviously caused some damage after all."

"Well we can't go back now, Mike," Browne said firmly. "See if you can get it back on line, will you. I don't want to get stuck into a bunch of Argies with no bloody radar!"

"Now just settle down, Prentice, and start talking slowly. You're not making any damned sense. Are you seriously telling me that the Argentineans are trying to sink the Royal Yacht?"

"Mr Ambassador," Prentice implored, "You've gotta believe me. It's this one guy, Captain Sanchar. He's the Commander of Number Three Wing at Puerta Belgrano. Ambassador, I left a brief with you two days ago on this whole thing."

"Yeah, well I've been out of my office," the Ambassador lied. "How the hell can you be sure he's not just going off to fly a routine mission?"

Prentice went over the whole story again, trying to be as patient as possible.

"OK, OK. Now look. If you're wrong and I end up looking a damned fool, you can kiss your pension goodbye. Understand, Prentice?"

"Yes Ambassador," Prentice replied wearily. It was not the first time that a superior had threatened the financial security of his old age.

"Now Prentice, you get down right away to Puerta Belgrano and see if you can talk to someone in authority. Take the chopper if you need to. The pilot's on standby in his flat in town. I'll get on to the Ministry of Defence, but whether I can find anyone senior enough to overrule a full Captain in command of a major base, I doubt very much indeed. You're just going to have to carry the ball yourself for a while. I'll call you on the car radio if I get anywhere."

"Thanks, Ambassador. I'm on my way," Prentice replied. On the way out of his office, he picked up his gun from the security cabinet.

Turnbull was pacing up and down the bridge, making everyone feel even more nervous. He had spoken on the satellite link to Sir Michael Townsend, who had promised at once to contact the Home Secretary. Turnbull had no doubt that the Prime Minister would be in the Cabinet Office within an hour, wherever he was. Despite the seriousness of the situation, he had to smile a little at the picture in his mind of the total panic his message would have caused.

"What's so funny?" Captain Morrison asked, bemused at the expression on his colleague's face.

"Nothing really, I just had a thought about the

London lot running round like headless chickens," Turnbull replied.

"You can say that again. Christ, nothing like this has happened for many a year. I hope this is all worthwhile and we're not barking up the wrong tree," Morrison added.

Turnbull shook his head. "There are just too many things pointing in the same direction. I can't believe all these threads don't tie up together in bloody big knot at Sanchar's base. The moment I looked in his eyes at Dublin airport I knew he was up to something."

"Thank heavens you did, Richard. No-one else seems to have taken it very seriously."

A call came up from the operations room. "We've got Mission Black Zero Three on the radio, sir. He'll be on time, but he's got some problem with his radar. Mount Pleasant have just contacted us as well. They're getting another Tornado off, but they now say it's going to be after five o'clock before he gets here."

"Bloody hell," Turnbull cursed, "the show could well be over by then."

"I've had a word with the Admiral on the Yacht," Morrison said. "He's decided to alert the Queen, just in case we do get any trouble. I've offered the Lynx to get the Royal party away from danger, but he doesn't think she'll be prepared to leave her ship and her crew. I think he's probably right too."

Turnbull nodded. "What do we do if Sanchar tries to do a Kamikaze on Britannia?"

"Difficult, to be absolutely honest," Morrison replied grimly. "We'll try to keep close to the Yacht and hope to shoot him down before he gets too close. I really feel like I'm boxing in the dark at the moment. We don't know for sure what type of aeroplane he'll be flying or even if he's likely to be carrying weapons."

"What's the worse possible case?" Turnbull asked.

"Super Etendard with Exocet," Morrison replied emphatically.

"But they've only got fourteen of them, all getting pretty old, and I can't imagine they'd be carrying live Exocets around in peacetime."

Remembering what Exocet missiles had done to Royal Navy ships during the Falklands War, Turnbull asked again what could be done in the event of an attack.

"Well we've got chaff and other electronic measures. The chaff is small slivers of metal that hopefully can confuse the radar in the missile. We can also try and shoot it down with our Seawolf missiles. But as we found during the Falklands War, Seawolf is mainly for self-protection, so he's got to be flying towards us. That's OK if we're between him and the Yacht, but if he manages to get round to the other side ... Let's hope he's got other plans."

∽

Prentice braked violently as he saw Reilly leaping out from the telephone booth at the side of the road. In the distance, through the rows of barbed wire, he could see the aircraft lined up on the apron. Reilly rushed up to him.

"They've just started up one of the aircraft. I can't see what it is, but I think it's about to taxi out."

"I'm going to see if I can get on the base," Prentice shouted. "There has to be someone in charge if they're flying."

"But you'll bust your cover," Reilly protested.

He was right. Prentice would never be able to claim again that he was merely an economic adviser.

"Look, buddy," he replied, "if this guy's doing what I think he is, we're all going to be busted - make no mistake about it."

Leaving the startled-looking Reilly, he raced off towards the main entrance to the Base, some two miles down the highway. As he pulled up in front of the gate, he was astonished to find a very red-faced Rosario remonstrating loudly with two armed naval policemen.

"But you fools, can't you read. I'm Inspector Rosario of the Buenos Aires Police. I must speak to the officer in charge at once. It is very urgent!"

The senior police guard was talking to someone on the telephone. He waited for a time whilst Rosario fumed, nodded a couple of times and put down the receiver.

"Commander Mantana has spoken to Chief Inspector Deron at Buenos Aires. They know nothing of your being here, senor, and the Base is at high security alert. If you do not leave at once, you will be placed under military arrest."

Prentice got out of the car. Rosario turned and his face exploded in rage. "You bastard, I told you to stay away from here."

He reached under his jacket and pulled out a gun, but before he could raise it one of the policemen hit him with a hefty blow on the back of his balding head. He dropped motionless on the ground. The guard raised his rifle towards Prentice.

"OK, OK, I'm going. I don't want any trouble," Prentice called out, realising the futility of trying to get on to the Base. Glad to leave Rosario for them to sort out, he drove back to the telephone box. As he got out of the car, a Mirage fighter roared overhead and banked sharply.

Prentice watched it intently. "Thank Christ," he said to himself, "it doesn't seem to be carrying any weapons. I hope I can raise the Ambassador."

Throwing a handful of loose change onto the plastic ledge in the booth, he tapped out the secret number that connected with the Ambassador's cell phone. It didn't even go as far as on ring before he heard a voice at the end.

"Yes."

"Ambassador, it's Prentice. I couldn't get on the Base; it's wrapped up as tight as a mummy's shroud. The local police inspector - a nasty character called Rosario - got himself laid out for trying too hard to get past the guard post."

The Ambassador interrupted him. "I've just spoken to the Minister of Defence and he's getting onto the Base right away. I'm not sure whether he believes any of it, but he's giving us the benefit of the doubt and is going to stop all flying until it's all sorted out."

"Too late for that, sir," Prentice said, "I've just watched a Mirage take off. But at least it wasn't carrying any weapons."

"That's something anyway. OK, Prentice stay ....." The Ambassador's voice was drowned out by the roar of a jet engine.

Prentice peered out of the booth and a look of horror came over his face. "Ambassador, Ambassador .... are you still there, sir?" he shouted over the noise.

"Yes of course I am. What the hell was all that noise?"

"Ambassador, you've gotta get onto the Brits right away. A Super Etendard has just got airborne, and I could see quite clearly - it's carrying an Exocet missile!"

Flight Lieutenant Curtis breathed a sigh of relief. "I've managed to get the radar back on line, sir," he reported.

"That's great, Mike! Well done," Browne called back over the intercom. They both knew that luck had played a greater part than skill in recovering the system, but their relief needed some expression. Browne called to advise the ship and the other Tornado that their weapons system was now fully serviceable. They sounded relieved. But he was getting a little anxious about the physical condition of the other crew. They were young and fit, but they'd been in the air a long time. The radio broke into life again.

"Mission Black Zero Two, remain on patrol until further notice. This instruction is from your senior authority."

The operations controller on HMS Cornwall had obviously been talking directly to Mount Pleasant. Under the circumstances the decision was understandable, but it increased Browne's concern. One accident on this Mission was already more than enough. He decided to have a word with the other crew.

"Zero Three to Zero Two; call me on Two Three Nine Decimal Five."

The other aircraft acknowledged and they changed radio channels to the Squadron "natter" frequency, where they could talk freely.

"Zero Three to Zero Two, how are you feeling?"

"Zero Two, no problems at present. Bladder's a bit full, but we want to stay to get a DFC as well."

Browne chuckled. "Roger Zero Two, but play it carefully, especially if we get down to low level. It'll be getting dark down there in half an hour."

They changed back to the Ship's radio frequency and confirmed that all was still quiet. It was three thirty.

∞

Mantana was having trouble keeping his cool. The Admiral calling from the Ministry of Defence was screaming at him almost hysterically.

"Admiral, I'm telling you that Captain Sanchar has already taken off. Yes, that's right, sir, he's airborne."

These non-flying sailors never seemed to understand anything about air operations.

"No, sir, I cannot call him back. He is at low level, outside radio cover. He'll be back in about an hour and I'll get him to call you then."

The Admiral's voice rose in pitch and strength. The colour drained out of Mantana's face as the Admiral went into detail.

"But Admiral, I cannot believe that. Captain Sanchar is flying a trial sortie; we have been planning it for weeks ...." Mantana's voice trailed away as several things suddenly clicked into place: Sanchar's insistence that he should fly the sortie himself, his specifying precisely the date and time, and his single-mindedness throughout the whole trial.

"Admiral, I can get another Mirage airborne, but we have no weapons fitted. It would take hours to get them out of store and onto the aircraft."

"Yes, sir, we will try to contact the Mirage that is already airborne. Yes, I understand, sir. He is to stop Captain Sanchar penetrating Uruguayan or Brazilian airspace at all costs. Yes, I understand what that means, sir. Of course, Admiral, when Captain Sanchar lands I'll have him put under close arrest. Yes, of course, sir, no-one is to leave the Base until you approve it."

Mantana put down the phone. He had known his Commanding Officer for fifteen years. They had been at flying school together, and had been through the Malvinas War on the same Squadron. And, Mantana knew, deep down, that if anyone could complete this action successfully, it was Jose Sanchar.

CHAPTER 17

All seemed well. The radar was working to perfection, the electronic jamming pod test had revealed no faults, and the Exocet missile status arrays showed green for 'go'. Sanchar descended to low level and turned left, away from the practice target, towards the North. He would be nearly forty miles away from the Mirage at his closest point during the long transit to the wide River Plate Estuary. That should be more than enough to avoid radar detection.

Sanchar checked his fuel and engine instruments carefully. He had a long way to go, and would need to fly the aircraft at economical speeds for the first few hundred miles. This would put him at risk in Argentinean waters, but would leave sufficient fuel in reserve to cope with the unexpected when he needed it most.

He was outside cover of ground-based radio at this height. However, he knew it wouldn't be long before Lieutenant Cano in his Mirage became suspicious. He would be expecting to make contact with the Super Etendard on his radar by now. Sanchar wasn't surprised when the radio call came.

"Pedro One Zero, Pedro One Zero, this is Black Cat Nine Nine. Do you read me ... over."

Sanchar ignored the call, but the next message froze his blood.

"Pedro One Zero from Black Cat Nine Nine, you are to pull up to ten thousand feet and return to base immediately. I say again, you are to pull up to ten thousand feet and return to base. This order is mandatory from high command. Acknowledge!"

Sanchar swore under his breath. Somehow the authorities had discovered his plan. Or perhaps they had picked up a few leads and were just guessing. Whatever, Sanchar knew that the Mirage would now be pursuing him. It was not armed, but if it found him it could relay his position to others, and possibly even alert the British. He descended a further fifty feet and accelerated to four hundred knots. At this speed he could still complete his attack, but would have little in reserve.

"Captain Sanchar, this is Black Cat Nine Nine. From high command, they are aware of your intentions. You are to turn back at once and land at Puerta Belgrano. Acknowledge."

Sanchar again kept silent. He knew that Cano would have his Direction Finder switched on, and just a touch on the radio transmitter button would instantly provide him with a magnetic bearing to the Super Etendard. And if they knew the approximate position of the Royal Yacht, it would be a simple matter for the Mirage pilot to plot a course that would give him a good chance of interception. Sanchar simply had to hope that he could outrun the fighter, or that at low level his dark grey camouflage would prove sufficient concealment. He decided that he would leave his jamming pod in standby mode for the moment. If he were to switch it on too early, it would give early warning to the British and might even attract the attention of any Brazilian or Uruguayan aircraft in the area. He looked nervously over his shoulder, but could see nothing in the sky behind him.

With a quick calculation, the operations staff at Puerto Belgrano had turned the Mirage on to an approximate heading to intercept Sanchar. Fifteen miles astern, Lieutenant Cano got the first indication of Sanchar's Super Etendard on his radar, and accelerated to five hundred knots. It was three thirty five.

∞

Even the normally ice-cool Morrison was having trouble keeping still on the bridge. It seemed that every head on the ship was turned to the south, scanning the skies. The Royal Yacht Britannia was at full speed, tucked under the starboard side of HMS Cornwall, as they took the most direct path towards the River Plate Estuary. Their cleverly designed route had taken them nearly eighty miles from the coast, and even at their present speed it would take four hours to reach the safety of the outer harbour, where they could tether up amongst the many ships before finally entering Montevideo the following morning. Turnbull found himself wondering if they would be making the final part of that journey or if, like HMS Sheffield, they would be turned to molten metal and sent to the bottom of the dark grey Atlantic.

"Captain, urgent message coming up from the communications room. They want to read it out in clear."

"Go ahead," Morrison replied, taking the handset from the radio officer. "Christ, OK got that," he said grimly.

He turned towards the others. "It's a Super Etendard alright, and he's got a live Exocet on board. That was the American Ambassador himself. Apparently the Argentine Minister of Defence knew nothing about this. It's obviously Sanchar's private war, but that's no great comfort to us".

He called down to the operations room. "Make sure the fighters get the message that it's definitely a Super Etendard, and it's armed with Exocet. And don't let either of them off patrol until I give the word."

Turnbull turned to Morrison, his face taut. "Can those Tornados stop Sanchar getting that missile off at us?" he asked.

"I hope so, Richard," he replied. "I bloody well hope so".

―∞―

Browne was taking fuel from the Tristar tanker when the call came from Black Zero Two.

"Possible contact. Long range, bearing one nine zero degrees."

"Clear to break," the tanker Captain called out over the radio, and Browne banked away from the Tristar rapidly, rolled over and pulled down towards the patrol area.

"Black Zero Two, now positive contact, bearing one nine zero degrees, low level. Could be a pair."

Browne called down to the ship, a little grey dot on the sea below. "Cornwall from Black Zero Three. Did you copy? Black Zero Two has contacts, possibly two, bearing one nine zero from you, low level."

The controller's voice came back with urgency. "Roger Zero Three. Intercept and if Argentinean you are cleared to destroy. Acknowledge."

"Roger. Understand if Argentinean, destroy. Did you copy Zero Two?"

The other fighter acknowledged, the crew's voices high with excitement.

"We're about ten miles behind Zero Two, sir," Curtis remarked. "I've got him painting on radar, but no sign of the targets yet. The bloody kit's still playing up a bit."

"OK, Mike," Browne replied quietly, "just get what you can out of it".

There was no point in getting his navigator rattled at this stage.

"Zero Two, now good contact with both targets. They're about five miles in trail and the rear contact has overtake."

"Roger Zero Two," Browne acknowledged. "Don't get sandwiched. Identify the rear man first. If he's Argentinean give him a Sidewinder and we'll take the front man out with Skyflash."

Browne knew that after the identification pass the other Tornado would be in the rear quadrant of the target, and so well placed to fire a lethal heat-seeking Sidewinder missile up his jet pipe. If Browne and Curtis got the attack profile right, they should then be able to fire a longer range radar-homing Skyflash missile directly at the front target. It all depended on whether Zero Two could get a successful and quick identification. They sped towards the interception point, Curtis crisply calling out the weapons checks which would ensure that both sets of missiles and the twenty seven millimetre Mauser cannon were primed and ready for the kill.

"OK, I'm getting intermittent contact with targets now," Curtis called out over the intercom. "They're still in trail, but the second target seems to be closing fast on the front man. They're only about two miles apart now."

"Come on Zero Two," Browne urged under his breath, "get stuck in to them both."

∞

Sanchar simultaneously switched on the radar and the radio homer, and pulled up quickly to two thousand feet. This made him vulnerable to detection by the escort fighters, but he could not pick up his target on radar at very low level. He let the scanner sweep once, then switched it off and examined the afterglow. As expected, there were over forty surface contacts, all heading towards the busy mouth of the River Plate. He anxiously watched the radio homer, which should give him the bearing to the target as soon as the concealed device started to transmit. Nothing ... damn...those people...he should never.... but suddenly the instrument sprang to life and the white needle jumped to twenty degrees right. They were further out from the coast than he had been expecting, which would give him an even greater problem with fuel. Banking steeply, he brought the indicator to show straight ahead, steadied briefly and gave the radar one more sweep. There, on the nose at sixty miles ... two contacts. Sanchar's heart leapt at the first tangible signs of his quarry. He had spent ten years preparing for this moment, and the scent of the kill made his pulse race. He now needed only to get sufficiently close to separate the targets on radar. The clearer picture would enable him to fly around the weapons cover provided by the escort ship and get a clear shot at the Royal Yacht herself.

Sanchar was forcing the aircraft down again to low level when he got the first sight in his rear view mirror of the fast-approaching Mirage. It was already at two miles, and as he accelerated to four hundred and fifty knots, he saw the flash of reheat from the pursuing fighter. He would be overtaken by the more nimble Mirage in less than a minute. God, thought Sanchar, he's going to try and ram me! In desperation he switched on the electronic jamming pod. As he did so, he was horrified to see the grey shape of a Royal Air Force Tornado F3 streaking past nearly a mile above.

In Mission Zero Two, the pilot, Flight Lieutenant Mervyn Fuller, saw both Argentinean aircraft at the same time as Sanchar flew past underneath.

"Zero Two, visual contact. The lead aircraft is a Super Etendard - looks armed under starboard wing. The rear aircraft is a Mirage. Attacking now."

All too late, Lieutenant Cano saw the Tornado turning in behind. In desperation, he broke hard towards his opponent, but as he did his blood turned cold as Fuller squeezed the trigger and sent a Sidewinder missile screeching towards the Mirage's red-hot jet-pipe. Cano pulled his aircraft harder than he had ever done in his life. The blood rushed to his head...his heart froze. As first he thought it would pass behind, but suddenly it loomed up on him, striking the fuselage behind the right wind root. The Mirage tumbled through the sky. The engine screamed...alarm bells clanged in his headphones. He tried desperately to reach the ejection handle, but the `g' forces flung him outwards against the straining seat harness. The last thing his bulging eyes ever saw was the crest of a dark wave as his stricken Mirage rolled inverted into the sea.

"Good kill on the Mirage," Fuller shouted triumphantly. "Low on fuel. Going to the Tanker."

Browne could now see the one remaining target on his radar repeater in the front cockpit.

"Shit," Curtis exclaimed in frustration as the radar flickered and then died.

"OK, Mike, see if you can get it back again," Browne said, "He's got a jammer on board as well. We'll have to try and get a visual kill on him."

"He should be on the nose about five miles," Curtis advised, frenetically working to get the system back on line.

"OK, Mike...got him visual," Browne shouted, and both men groaned as he pulled the Tornado round in a six `G' turn towards the Super Etendard.

Sanchar picked up the second Tornado as it turned in towards him. It was already close to missile release range, and he started firing off decoy flares to reduce Browne's chance of a successful Sidewinder firing. Going to full power, he pulled up hard into the layers of cloud at three thousand feet.

"Bugger it," Browne cried in frustration. "I couldn't get a good shot off with those flares…he's just pulled into cloud. Mike, we've got to get that radar back."

"Yeah, I'm trying, sir, but the bloody thing's not playing ball."

"Cornwall, this is Zero Three. One Mirage destroyed, one Super Etendard heading towards you from the south, range about thirty miles. Zero Two is going to the tanker."

"Roger Zero Three. This is Cornwall. We hold him contact, with you five miles in trail. Can you attack?"

"Zero Three, problem with radar. Target is in cloud. We'll do our best Cornwall."

"Roger, he's now turning starboard and heading zero three zero degrees, range twenty to us."

Sanchar was turning away from the surface force. He was pretty sure now that the nearest target was the frigate, and he was flying at maximum speed to mount his attack from the other side, where the Yacht would be easy prey. To his relief the Tornado's radar was not showing on his warning receiver. It was obviously a stroke of luck, but to be sure he would stay in cloud for a little longer yet. But only a little longer. He noticed with alarm that the fuel had been guzzled quicker than he had expected during the skirmish with the Tornado, and he would certainly have only one chance to launch his missile.

On board HMS Cornwall, Turnbull's knuckles were white as he gripped the rail around the bridge. "What's he doing now?" he asked Morrison.

"My God, he's trying to get round to the north. We're going to have to switch sides."

Both ships swung towards each other, as Sanchar turned hard back in on his attack run.

"Fire chaff now," Morrison ordered to the operations room, and with a series of bangs, several cartridges of metallic needles were blasted into the sky to form a protective curtain around the Royal Yacht.

Sanchar was in the process of dropping out of cloud when his radar picture became confused as the chaff obscured both targets. Frantically, he adjusted the controls and manoeuvred his aircraft to give the system a better chance of reacquiring the Royal Yacht. But as the range rapidly closed, he realised his task was becoming more hopeless. Scanning the horizon visually, for the first time he saw her. There silhouetted against the dark skyline, was the Britannia. And manoeuvring rapidly in front of her was a Type 22 Frigate.

As Sanchar came out of cloud, Morrison and Turnbull both shouted together and pointed to the rapidly closing aircraft. Without warning, the whole ship shook as a Seawolf surface to air missile left its cocoon and sped towards the Super Etendard at hypersonic speed.

Detecting the threat at once, Sanchar broke hard away from the missile and gritted his teeth in anticipation of the sickening jar of an explosion. Miraculously, the Seawolf fell just short and detonated on the wave tops, sending a shower of spray up to meet him as he pulled back up into cloud, heading towards the west. He tapped the fuel gauge; it was almost empty. The Tornado was in hot pursuit, and his warning receiver told him that the Foxhunter radar was now scanning him menacingly. He could not turn back without risking a Sidewinder in his jet pipe. Survival forced him to do what he most hated - run away. With tears streaming down his face, and his shoulders shaking with rage, he took up a heading for the coast of southern Brazil.

CHAPTER 18

After the frenetic activity of the previous hour, the sudden calm took them all by surprise.

"Where's he gone?" Turnbull asked.

Without replying, Morrison picked up the handset on the internal communications panel and spoke briefly to the operations officer. He turned and faced Turnbull, the relief evident on his face.

"He's disappeared into Brazilian air space. It looks as though he's run out of fuel and has headed towards some sort of safe haven. The Tornado has hauled off and has gone back to the Tanker."

"Thank God," Turnbull sighed. "I wonder if he's going to land somewhere or if he'll have to bale out."

"I can't imagine he's going to be very popular anywhere, least of all in the territory of the official hosts of his intended victims," Morrison replied, dryly. Somehow he had managed to regain his composure.

A white-faced young seaman brought in a tray of steaming coffee. Morrison declined, but Turnbull needed something to relieve his dry mouth and throat. To his embarrassment, his hands were shaking so much that he slopped most of the liquid onto the bridge floor. With a lot of effort he managed to hold the cup to his lips just long enough to take a quick scalding gulp.

"That's why I didn't have any." Morrison muttered discreetly.

"First Sea Lord on the satellite link for you, sir," the

communications officer called out.

"Crikey," Morrison said, subconsciously straightening his tie, "I can't believe this is my medal already."

He picked up the black receiver. "Morrison, sir. Good afternoon, sir." He winked at Turnbull. "Yes, a fairly exciting afternoon, sir. I think so, sir, he appears to have gone to try and bale out or land in Brazil. Yes, we did have a go, Sir. Just one Seawolf, but it fell short. No, they got the Mirage, but couldn't shoot down the Super Etendard...yes, I agree sir. No, they're both back on the tanker now, but I think the show's over. Thank you, sir... yes, I'll pass that on to the ship's company."

He put the telephone down. "We seem to have done well, gentlemen."

Squadron Leader Browne acknowledged reluctantly. "Roger, understood. We're to stay with the tanker for thirty minutes before resuming patrol. Cornwall, any news on Black Zero Four? Black Zero Two is way beyond maximum crew fatigue time and should return to base."

"Roger, Zero Three from Cornwall. Zero four has had some problem after take-off and has landed again at Mount Pleasant. He is delayed two hours. From the Commander, threat now seems to have disappeared, so Zero Two may return to base."

With obvious relief and understandable jubilance, Zero Two banked steeply to the left, and with a large black smudge marking the spot under the wing where the Sidewinder had once been housed, he turned onto a heading for the Falkland Islands.

"Christ, I feel pissed off about not getting that bastard," Curtis muttered abjectly.

"Yeah, me too," Browne replied. "Still, he didn't get to

the Yacht. I suppose that's the main thing."

Curtis was clearly not convinced, but he kept his annoyance to himself. The crew of the Tristar were tucking into a tasty-looking snack, and as usual they held up their fare to gloat at the fighter crew.

"That's all they've got going for them." Curtis muttered. "They must have been hacked off sitting up here listening to all that going on."

"They do a good job," Browne reminded his young navigator. "I wouldn't let my daughter marry a tanker pilot though," he added.

The operations controller on the frigate disturbed their chattering. "Zero Three this is Cornwall. From coastal air defences, they have not picked up the Super Etendard, but a chopper has sighted a fuel slick and some floating wreckage a few miles off the coast. It looks as though he ran out of fuel. Stay with the tanker for a further fifteen minutes, then resume routine patrol."

"Roger Zero Two," Browne acknowledged. "Well, Mike, that looks as though that's it. I think I'll make a start on those chicken sandwiches."

∞

Sanchar pulled himself together with difficulty. He might still have a chance. The Tornado had turned away as he entered Brazilian airspace, and so far there had been no sign of Brazilian fighters. With a little luck, their air defence radars had not picked him up at such low level, and although he knew they must have been alerted by now, they would find plotting his precise position virtually impossible. The sun was dipping down below the horizon, but there was still sufficient light to see the ground and make a successful landing. Good fortune had taken him to the coast south of Rio Grande, a few miles north of the border with Uruguay. Many years before, he and a friend had landed at a small airfield on the coast. He had quickly checked his flight handbook, and had confirmed that the runway was just long enough for a Super Etendard to land. Most importantly, they stored fuel for visiting business executive jets. They would not have much, but it would be more than enough to fill his fuselage tanks. To save fuel he had jettisoned his nearly empty underwing tank ten miles out to sea, where it had subsequently been discovered by the Brazilian helicopter. Without the balancing effect of the fuel tank, the asymmetry of the single Exocet missile made flight uncomfortable. But with care, the aircraft could still be flown safely and effectively at all speeds.

As the coastline passed by under him, Sanchar pulled up, happy that he was now safe from radar detection. In the distance he could see the shimmering surface of Lake Mirim, and turning slowly left he identified his position as ten miles north of the small airfield. He dared not risk calling them up on the radio, as it would almost certainly give them time to call in the local police or military. It was unlikely, he reasoned, that anyone else would be flying at this time, as most business travellers would already have left, and any club enthusiasts would have landed well before sunset.

The fuel low level warning light flashed at him again, but he calculated he just had enough to make it. He brought the speed back to two hundred knots, keeping the coast five miles on his left side, and strained his eyes forward to try and pick up the landing site. When he finally did see it, it was too late to make a safe approach, and he was forced to fly one tight orbit to reduce speed further and lower the flaps and undercarriage. As expected, there were no lights on the airfield, but he could, by straining his eyes just make out the narrow concrete strip in the twilight. Rolling out on finals, he selected full flap and reduced speed to one hundred and fifty knots. He touched down firmly, exactly on the end of the runway, and braked as hard as he could to avoid running off the other end into the rocky overshoot area. The aircraft slewed viciously under the strain, but he managed to keep close to the centreline, and came to a jerky halt with only fifty metres of concrete remaining. Carefully, he turned round, repositioned on the centre of the runway and applied the parking brake. The fuel gauge showed empty, but the engine kept turning smoothly. He dared not close down, for to do so would mean a protracted start-up procedure which he had at all costs to avoid. Time was critical, not only to press home his attack before Britannia slipped into the busy waterway of the River Plate estuary, but also to take off again before the local police arrived on the scene. In peacetime, the fire risk from refuelling with a jet engine running was too high, but he was at war and safety was low on his priorities.

It seemed an eternity before a black station wagon, marked `airport manager', arrived on the runway beside him. It was shortly followed by an ancient red fire engine. A very bald man climbed out of the station wagon and began gesticulating wildly.

Carefully avoiding the jet intakes, Sanchar leapt out of the cockpit, peeled off his flying gloves and helmet, and extended his hand in greeting.

"My sincere apologies, senor. Captain Sanchar of the Argentine Navy," he said in fluent Portuguese.

"Never mind your damned apologies," the furious airport manager shouted back, "what the hell do you think you're doing just landing your jet...."

He was cut short as Sanchar got close enough to grab him by the throat and pull out his automatic pistol. The man gasped in surprise as Sanchar forced him to the ground and turned his gun on the advancing fire crew.

"Tell your men to get back or I'll blow your bloody brains out," he snarled.

The manager hesitated and Sanchar fired the gun into the ground an inch from his right ear.

"Get back, get back," he screamed in terror, his eardrums shattered,

"Now listen carefully, senor. You have five minutes exactly to get a jet fuel bowser over here. I'm starting my watch now, and for every minute after four twenty, I'll put a bullet into your legs."

The manager sobbed, his hands clamped to his ears. Sanchar pulled him round.

"Do it," he shouted, raising the pistol again. It had the desired effect.

"Speak to air traffic control," he shouted hoarsely to the fire crew. "Get them to send the jet bowser now... now!"

One of the firemen muttered something to his colleagues and started to walk towards Sanchar. Taking aim carefully, Sanchar shot him in the left kneecap. The man went down screaming, blood oozing from under his protective fire suit. One of the others scrambled to the vehicle and blurted out a message to the control tower. In the distance, Sanchar could see frenzied activity, and he had no doubt that the police would be on their way. But the nearest village was about ten miles away, and over the rough roads it would take at least twenty minutes for them to arrive. With luck he would already be airborne.

Forty-five seconds before the five minutes were up, a green fuel bowser trundled unsteadily across the grass towards them. Sanchar cursed as he saw that it was even smaller than he had feared. He waved his gun to hurry them along. Two very frightened mechanics jumped out and looked for instructions from the forlorn manager.

"Fill the aircraft up, and do it quickly," Sanchar ordered.

"The engine is still running," one of the mechanics protested.

"Do it," the airport manager shouted, his voice choking as Sanchar stood firmly on the back of his neck.

Far more slowly than Sanchar would have liked, the two men hitched up the fuel bowser to the aircraft connector and started to fill the tanks. He was acutely aware of time passing, and of the darkening of the skies.

"You," he called out to one of the firemen. "Tell air traffic control to switch on the runway and perimeter lights. And tell them to leave them on."

"One thousand kilogram's," one of the mechanics called out, starting to disconnect the hose from the aircraft.

"That's not enough. Keep putting it in," Sanchar ordered.

The man shrugged his shoulders, and started the fuel flowing again. After a couple of minutes, the flow stopped.

"One thousand six hundred kilogram's. You've had all you're going to get, senor."

It should be just enough, Sanchar thought.

"All of you get in your vehicles, keep your headlights on, and drive over to the tower. If you double back, or put your lights out, these two die. Now move!"

The men needed no second bidding and sped off leaving the airport manager and the injured fireman, who lay groaning in pain on the bloodstained grass. Sanchar waited until they were over halfway to the tower, and ordered the airport manager to stand up.

"You stay exactly where you are until I take off. If

I see any attempt to move away, I'll shoot you both. Understand?"

The man nodded. Sanchar kept his gun ready, and climbed back into the aircraft. It was now completely dark, but he could see the manager and the fireman clearly in the glow from the runway lights. Forcing himself to move efficiently to maximise every second, he strapped himself into the ejection seat, and left the canopy open until he had completed his pre-take off checks. As the glass dome closed over his head, he saw the airport manager dive into the darkness. Urgently, Sanchar ran the engine up to full power, and released the brakes. As the Super Etendard leapt forward, the ghostly figure of the manager appeared from the shadows fifty metres down the runway. Suicidally, he lurched drunkenly towards the aircraft, a large object held high above his head. As the aircraft lights picked him out more clearly, Sanchar saw a look of pure hatred on the man's face as with every ounce of his strength he threw a fire extinguisher towards the nose of the aircraft. Sanchar instinctively ducked as it struck the radome and bounced off the windscreen, leaving it scratched but unbroken. As he re-focused his eyes back onto the night outside, the runway lights extinguished, leaving only pitch blackness ahead. He tried desperately to keep straight, but suddenly there was a jarring bang as the left mainwheel went off the side of the runway and burst in the rocky ground. For a moment he thought he would crash, but just as it seemed the aircraft would shake itself to pieces, it gained enough speed to claw its way into the air. Away from the ground, the vibration ceased. But he had no doubt that there would be a lot of damage around the burst mainwheel. Against his better judgement, he raised the undercarriage, and was relieved to see the cockpit indicator showing it all properly stowed and locked. He would never need to lower the undercarriage again, and the high aerodynamic drag with the wheels stuck down would have drastically cut down on his available top speed. Carefully banking the aircraft he headed towards the coast.

As he rolled level, the radar warning system alarmed and showed an immediate threat in his tail quadrant. Sanchar swore out loud. Sure enough, there in the rear view mirror, he could just make out the flashing navigation lights of two aircraft. They were closing very fast, and from their behaviour he had no doubt that they were fully armed interceptors of the Brazilian Air Force. Quickly he switched on the electronic jamming pod, dropped down to low level, and jettisoned a stream of chaff to confuse their radars. After gathering a bit more speed he pulled back on the control column. The aircraft bucked violently, and came close to stalling as the speed dropped desperately low during the steep climb. From nearly three miles above he looked down to see the lights of the interceptors as they searched for him out towards the coast. It had worked; the Brazilian pilots had failed to detect his rapid climb out of the cloud of chaff. Picking a safe heading, Sanchar dived back down to low level to avoid detection by the main air defence radars. After ensuring that the fighters were still ten miles away over the coast, he turned south towards the nearby Uruguayan border.

Captain Sanchar was back in business, and this time no-one was going to stop him completing his mission.

CHAPTER 19

Captain Morrison's eyes opened wide as he listened to the message from the operations room.

"Christ almighty! OK, make sure that the Tornado is moved over to the west. Oh, good, well done. Sound Action Stations!"

The alarm bell sounded around the ship, and the men who thought that the danger was past came scurrying back out of their rest areas.

"What the hell's happening now?" Turnbull asked.

"We've had an unconfirmed report from the Brazilian coastguard that an Argentinean aircraft landed at an airfield near the Rio Grande. Apparently the pilot held the place to ransom, got his aircraft refuelled and took off about ten minutes ago."

"My God," Turnbull exclaimed, "it's got to be Sanchar! He's bloody determined alright."

Morrison picked up his radio headpiece and spoke a few words to the Admiral on the Royal Yacht.

"That's what I reckon, sir, so we'll switch now and put you on our port side. Yes, sir, the Tornado is being repositioned." He laughed weakly. "We'll try to get things back to normal as soon as possible, sir."

He turned to Turnbull. "Apparently, the Royal Party are getting fed up with having their bridge game disturbed!"

The brief burst of humour did little to ease the growing tension on the bridge. Morrison spoke briefly to his logistics and armament specialists and confirmed that they still had plenty of chaff to counter the Super Etendard's attack radar.

"God, I wish we had another Tornado or two overhead," he said. "I feel bloody vulnerable sitting here with only one aircraft for protection. Any news on Mission Black Zero Four?"

"No, sir," the communications officers replied. "I've been on to Mount Pleasant and they're still working on a take-off time of five o'clock."

"That means he won't be here for nearly two bloody hours," Morrison said in exasperation.

"Ops room for you, sir."

"Thanks," Morrison replied, snatching the handset. "Righto, let me know if you or the Tornado get sight of anything at all."

He turned back to Turnbull. "He's confirmed airborne alright! The Brazilians have got two fighters looking for him, but it seems he gave them the slip. The coastguard have spoken to the airfield he landed at, and they're just as anxious to get hold of him as we are. Apparently he shot a fireman and nearly killed the airport manager. He's certainly got the bit between his teeth."

Turnbull stared towards the dull glow of the coastline in the distance, and wondered what sort of man it took to give up ten years of his life in pursuit of revenge.

※

A half moon glowed dimly through the light cloud and cast a soft sheen over the dark waters of Lake Mirim. Sanchar took advantage of the better light conditions and descended to less than a hundred feet. He had decided to stay over the Lake until well inside Uruguayan territory. There were only a few fishermen out, and anyway they would almost certainly have no way of making contact with the shore. Hopefully the Brazilians would have decided not to expose their embarrassment at failing to intercept him to their Uruguayan neighbours. Once across the border, he expected little defensive activity.

On his map he had recalculated the new position of the Royal Yacht. They would undoubtedly be making for the River Plate at full speed, and he reckoned that they would not have bothered with time consuming evasive tactics. Assuming the homing device was still working, he should be able to pick them up outside the busy sea lanes. Although he was a naval pilot, Sanchar knew well enough how the frigate Captain's mind would be working. He would know by now that Sanchar had taken off again from the Brazilian mainland, and would be expecting him to come in from the west.

"Well, my friend," Sanchar thought, "I will not oblige you this time."

He would continue south until he broke out over the sea at the mouth of the River Plate, and then circle around to attack from the south east. If he had double-guessed the British correctly, this would put the escort frigate and any fighters on the wrong side and leave the Yacht wide open to attack.

Squadron Leader Browne tried hard to conceal his impatience. "Yes, OK Mike, I know it's not your fault, but see what you can do will you."

The radar was causing problems again, and Curtis's best efforts had failed to sort it out this time. The urgent warning that they could expect a further attack from the West had increased Browne's frustration. Without radar, he could not use his best weapon, the lethal Skyflash radar-homing missile. Worse, in the dark he would be hard-pressed, even with help from Cornwall's radar, to get a visual pick up on the low-flying Super Etendard. He looked up at the thinning cloud above. With some luck they might get a bit of help from the moon, but it would need a lot of luck to get into a position where he could fire Sidewinders or the Mauser gun.

Curtis grunted in frustration. "Well, I'm getting something out of it," he said, "but I don't think it's going to be much use, sir."

"That's all we need," Browne groaned, "a mad Argentinean on the loose with an Exocet, and we've got a duff radar. I hope he plays ball and gives us a chance."

∞

"OK, let's get him into the overhead then," Morrison ordered, "at least then we can give him close control from our own radar."

"Problems?" Turnbull asked.

"I'm afraid so. The Tornado took a lightning strike after take off from Mount Pleasant and it's obviously damaged his radar. I've told the operations room to bring him into the overhead so we can give him the best chance of completing an interception."

"How's he going to do that with no radar?" Turnbull asked.

"Well, our radar controller will try and talk him onto the target. It's a bit like the days of Spitfires and Hurricanes, I suppose."

"Ye Gods," Turnbull replied, "twenty million pounds worth of aircraft and we're back to Second World War tactics."

"Don't worry, Richard," Morrison said, "after all we didn't do too badly then did we?"

"Call from London for you, sir," the communications man called out to Turnbull. "Sir Michael Townsend."

"Oh my God," Turnbull groaned, "what the hell's he doing at work over the weekend?"

Reluctantly, he sat down behind the communications panel and picked up the long distance radio headset. "Turnbull, sir."

"Richard, this is Sir Michael Townsend. Do you read me, over."

"Loud and clear, sir, over," Turnbull replied, playing along with Townsend's exaggerated radio procedures.

"The PM's asked for the latest on this Sanchar chap," Townsend's voice crackled through the headphones.

"Not much I can tell you, sir. It seems he's airborne again, but we haven't had any sight of him yet, over."

"What time are you expecting the attack? Over."

Turnbull raised his eyebrows in disbelief. "I can't predict that, sir, we don't know where he is...over"

"Well, I'm not sure I can tell the PM that, over."

This was more than Turnbull could stand. "Well, sir, I suggest you tell the PM that the Royal Navy and the Royal Air Force are doing their bloody best, and we'll let you know when the job's finished. Over and out!"

He slammed the receiver down. There was an embarrassed silence on the bridge.

"Oops," Morrison murmured.

"Shit, that's the end of my O.B.E" Turnbull whispered.

∞

Sanchar watched the town of Tocha slip past ten miles on his left side, its street lights twinkling in the distance. It was hard to imagine that so many people were out there, carrying on their normal lives, as he roared through the blackness intent on murder. Ahead of him he could just make out the lights of the port of Maldonado, and to the right the distant glow of the capital city of Montevideo. The fuel was holding out well. As expected there had been no sign of Uruguayan fighter aircraft, which had enabled him to fly at an economical cruising speed. A mile short of Maldonado, he turned left to avoid overflying populated areas. After a few minutes, he climbed on a north-easterly heading to ten thousand feet right underneath one of the main airways leading out from Montevideo. The civilian air traffic controllers would be paying no attention to outbound traffic and would almost certainly miss him. And with a bit of luck the radar operators on the escort frigate would confuse him with the stream of airliners above, even assuming that they were even bothering to look so far down to the south.

The coastline passed by below, and Sanchar throttled back to a slower speed to add to the deception. Up above him, a Boeing 747 Jumbo Jet continued its cruise climb to thirty-eight thousand feet. The passengers would just be settling back to enjoy their first meal of the journey, Sanchar reflected. Down below, the dark sea was covered with the bright pinpricks of sea vessels of all sizes. The radar screen in front of him remained blank. He had decided to leave it at standby for as long as possible, as it was even more important now to avoid alerting the escort frigate of his position. He had sat alongside sailors in operations rooms, and knew that they would be hunched over the myriad electronic devices, hoping for any clue which would reveal the enemy's position.

But the homing receiver was a passive system, and so could be used without alerting the ship's vigilant crew. Sanchar calculated he was now within one hundred miles of the Royal Yacht, and holding his breath he switched it on. At once the display illuminated and the needle moved hard to the left. Slowly, he descended down to sea level, replicating the profile of an airliner, and avoiding carefully any change of heading or speed that might arouse suspicion. Only when he was sure that he was below cover of Cornwall's radar did he turn and accelerate towards his target.

∞

The solitary Tornado was cruising several thousand feet above HMS Cornwall. The ship's lights were just visible below and the soft moon glinted off the white foam from the creamy bow wave.

"Cornwall from Mission Black Zero Three. Any further information?"

"Mission Zero Three from Cornwall, negative. How's the fuel?"

"Zero Three. We're OK for about another fifteen minutes, then we'll head for the tanker. Any news on Zero Four?"

"Affirmative, we've had his airborne time, and he'll be on task at about six-thirty."

Browne breathed a sigh of relief. "Thank God," he muttered, "My backside's killing me. I think I must be getting too old for this job, Mike."

Curtis was too concerned with the problems of his radar to be jovial. He had struggled for the past hour to get the system operating, but the damage done by the lightning strike now seemed to have had terminal results. Still, he thought it wouldn't be too long before their replacement arrived, after which they could hightail it home and get the radar fixed well in time for the return trip to the UK. He looked over the canopy rail as the aircraft banked to the left, and had a clear view of both Cornwall and Britannia heading towards the distant lights of the River Plate Estuary.

As Curtis watched the two ships, the radar controller two miles below yawned and rubbed his tired eyes. When he refocused back on the cathode ray tube he caught sight of a fading target return well out to the south east. He watched attentively, but the return didn't reappear. It could have been spurious......On the other hand......

"Sir," he called to the operations officers. "It may be nothing, sir, but I think I got a brief radar contact way down to the south east."

"OK, keep a close watch. I'll start moving Zero Three down in that direction just in case."

The operations controller had a brief conversation with the bridge and then repositioned the Tornado towards the south. As he did, the radar operator gave his full attention to the radar screen. For a while there was nothing. Suddenly, Sanchar's aircraft broke cover from behind the concealment of the earth's horizon. The operator's heart leaped.

"Contact, high speed, low level, bearing one three zero degrees. Now closing to range thirty."

"Christ!" the ops controller shouted. "Get the Tornado onto him quickly. Full close control." He picked up the headset to the bridge. "Sir, contact south easterly, less than thirty, coming towards. The Tornado's on his way to intercept."

"Roger," Morrison replied urgently.

He picked up the ship's Tannoy microphone.

"Air Attack Red, Air Attack Red." He swore as he turned to look at Turnbull. "The bastard's coming in from the other side."

Urgently he called the Royal Yacht and started the slow manoeuvre to cross to the other side. But he knew he would not have time, and unless the Tornado could stop him, Sanchar would have a clear view of Britannia. She would be a sitting duck.

As Sanchar pulled up to two thousand feet to prepare to launch the Exocet, he saw the reheat of the Tornado as the controller desperately talked Browne in to a firing position. He accelerated to full power... just a few switch selections...Exocet ready. On his radar, he could clearly see that the ships were trying to cross over. Too late. He licked his dry lips. He had them this time...too late to turn their Seawolf missiles towards him. His heart beat faster.

Browne was swearing and shouting at Cornwall's radar controller as he searched the black sea below him for the unseen Super Etendard.

"On the nose range two miles, still closing." The controller's shrill voice betrayed his fear.

Browne was just about to shout again for more information, when he caught the briefest glimpse of a slight glow against the sea. It faded then re-appeared, and Browne realised it was the reflection of the radar screen in Sanchar's aircraft against the canopy. Before it faded again, he brought the weapons sight onto the dim light and squeezed the trigger. The whole sky lit up in front of him as the Sidewinder roared off, sniffing for its prey.

Sanchar was in the final stages of preparing for the launch of the Exocet when the heat seeking missile violently struck the tail of his aircraft. The shock threw him sideways. Blood dripped in front of his right eye. He shook his head. The wounded Super Etendard began to yaw viciously to the right. Keep the nose up... full left rudder...keep it flying. His breath was coming in short gasps, but he knew he was nearly there. The attack seconds timer was counting down: ten, nine, eight...!

"Christ, he's still flying," Browne shouted in amazement.

"Give him another missile quickly," Curtis yelled.

Browne squeezed the trigger...another Sidewinder roared off towards its target. A second before it struck home Sanchar fired his remaining string of infra-red decoys and the missile flew harmlessly after them into the sea. But Browne was ready for this and sent both his last two Sidewinders in a salvo. "Got the bastard this time!" Browne yelled.

The missiles headed directly for the Super Etendard's tail area, but just before they reached their target, Browne watched in horror as the Exocet streaked away in a blaze of light and smoke.

"For Alfredo," Sanchar shouted above the noise, as the missile sped away towards the lights of the Royal Yacht. Before the smoke had cleared from in front of him, the two Sidewinders impacted, blowing apart the Super Etendard's rear fuselage.

After bouncing twice on the sea, it rose up into the South Atlantic sky in flames and disintegrated in a ball of fire.

"Cornwall from Zero Three. Exocet in the air! I say again Exocet in the air. Kill on the Super Etendard!"

"Roger, Zero Three, from Cornwall. Can you intercept the Exocet?"

"Wait one," Browne replied. "Shit, Mike, I can't see a bloody thing."

Ahead he could see the lights of the Royal Yacht getting closer. Beyond, but with no chance of bringing her Seawolf missiles to bear or to fire a protective cloud of chaff, was HMS Cornwall.

"OK, sir. I've just about got it on radar. Five degrees left at two miles. Go maximum speed."

Browne engaged full reheat and jettisoned his external fuel tanks to lighten his aircraft. The Tornado rocketed to well above the speed of sound.

"The target's intermittent and I can't lock the radar up for a Skyflash firing, sir. Can you get a visual and take it with guns?"

"I hope so, Mike. Keep talking...for Christ's sake, keep talking!"

The Royal Yacht was now only ten miles in front and closing fast.

"Got it, Mike! I can see the jet wake in the water. Check range now."

"Half a mile. Well inside range. Shoot! Shoot!"

Browne brought the gunsight onto the black area in front of the fluorescent jet wake and opened fire. The twenty seven millimetre cannon thumped away between his feet and tracer licked out into the blackness.

"Christ, the Yacht's only two miles. Target five hundred yards. We're too close ... it'll blow us all to pieces. Cease fire! Cease fire and break away!" Curtis shouted desperately.

Browne saw the ugly forebody of the missile silhouetted against the lights of the Royal Yacht and adjusted his aim. He was now staring down the flaming rocket motor. His gun spat out one last burst......

The crew on board the Britannia watched in horror as the missile and fighter bore down on them. As the Tornado's bullets tore into the Exocet, the whole sky suddenly lit up, and they dived for cover as burning fuel and exploding bits of metal showered across the decks.

In the dark night, the silence was eerie. The fires on the Royal Yacht had all been extinguished and the damage to her hull and superstructure had been assessed as superficial. The only sound was from the gentle thudding of the helicopter's rotors as it searched the dark waters for signs of life.

"OK, call it a day," Morrison said into his headset. He turned to Turnbull. "They've picked up Sanchar. He's in a very bad way. There's no sign of the Tornado crew. God, if they hadn't shot that Exocet down…."

Turnbull nodded and put his hand on Morrison's shoulder. "Can I go and see him?" he asked.

"Yes, let's go and meet the chopper," Morrison replied.

They walked down to the stern of the frigate and waited by the flight deck as the Lynx came to the hover and gently settled down. A doctor and the first aid team rushed forward to help lift out the stretcher. Carefully, they laid it down on the cold metal deck. As Turnbull knelt down and looked once again into Sanchar's eyes, he could see the man was dying.

"I said we'd meet again Captain," Turnbull whispered.

Sanchar opened his eyes and clutched at Turnbull's hand. His bruised lips moved slowly. Turnbull lowered his head to hear what he was saying.

Sanchar's voice came in gasps.

"Did I sink…sink the Britannia….kill the Queen?" He looked imploringly at his captors.

Turnbull held Morrison back. He looked down at this man…this man who had given up everything. God, he couldn't let him die like this….he was worth a thousand of that bastard Townsend.

"Yes, you did. You sank her," Turnbull replied quietly.

Sanchar smiled and slowly closed his eyes. As the light of the moon began to fade, he saw his brother, Alfredo, walking across the deck to take him into his arms.

CHAPTER 20

There was very little in the newspapers in either Argentina or Great Britain about the incident. The two governments had agreed to play the whole business down, and frantic activity on both sides had ensured that nosey journalists came to dead ends wherever they turned. Careers had been assured or threatened; money had changed hands and a few backs had been pressed against walls. It would probably leak out in the end, of course, but the official line would be that it was all a storm in a teacup....a misunderstanding, and no more. Relations between London and Buenos Aires had been improving, trade relations had been extended, and nobody wanted to upset the applecart.

As far as the Argentine Navy was concerned, Sanchar had been killed on a practice Exocet firing. It was an accident. His body had been returned to Argentina through the Uruguayan authorities, and he had been buried at sea with full military honours near the final resting place of the General Belgrano. Some who were present said that during the minute silence, the deep rumble of the old ship's mighty engines could be heard above the lapping of the waves. Others later said in whispers that as the body hit the water it appeared to be pulled down by wispy figures from the deep. But no-one took such stories too seriously.

∽

Inspector Rosario wiped his dirty red handkerchief across

his perspiring forehead. He winced as he touched the still tender lump on the side of his head where the guard's rifle had laid him flat for two hours. He would get that little bastard back one day. That is, he reflected, if he survived this interview with the Chief of Police. The door opened.

"Come in, inspector," the young police sergeant said brightly. Rosario shambled in and squared up to Chief of Police Bernardo Domez.

He was obviously furious. "Inspector Rosario, I have just returned from the Minister's officer. I need hardly tell you that he gave me a roasting. What the hell have you been up to Rosario?"

The inspector shrugged his shoulders. "Senor, I have done nothing unusual. I was merely making a few enquiries about this Sanchar after a tip-off that he might be planning some sort of anti-government activity."

"Hmm. And where did you get your....tip-off?" Domez enquired sarcastically.

"One of my officers heard something or other, senor. It was no more than that." Rosario was feeling very hot and uncomfortable.

"And what exactly did your officer hear, and from whom?" The Chief of Police's eyes were boring into Rosario.

"Er, well, senor....it was only rumour. I didn't give it too much thought. One of my men was following it up."

"Then why did you personally turn up at the airbase and demand entry, Inspector?"

Rosario was sweating profusely. His tongue was swollen in his throat. He tried to speak, but could only choke on his words. Behind him he heard the door open softly.

"I see you have trouble speaking, Inspector. You appear to need some help. I think you have a lot more to tell me yet."

He nodded and Rosario gasped as a rubber truncheon came down hard on the back of his head. His knees buckled; the truncheon struck again and he drifted into unconsciousness.

When Rosario recovered some three hours later, it was with a violent shock as a bucket of freezing water was thrown over his naked body. He gagged and fought for breath under the coarse sackcloth that covered his face. He was hanging from both arms, and the chains that bound him were biting deep into his fleshy wrists. Suddenly the world lit up as the bag was pulled off his head. Dank, warm breath hit him in the face. His eyes slowly focused on the familiar figure.

"Benitez!" he croaked in disbelief.

Sergeant Benitez roared with laughter. "Yes, my dear Inspector. But why do you look so surprised. Surely you didn't think you were the only one to use my little place in the country, senor?"

"Yes, but damn it all, Turnbull, that gives you no right to be impertinent. You have no idea what sort of pressure I was under while you were galavanting around the South Atlantic with the Navy." Sir Michael Townsend looked very hurt.

"Might I respectfully suggest, sir," Turnbull replied through clenched teeth, "that you were under far less pressure than those of us who were close to losing our lives."

"Oh, poppycock," Townsend snorted. "I've seen the

official report and it was all a busted flush.....an anti-climax. As usual, you're just blowing the whole business up, and I'm not prepared....."

He was cut short as Turnbull banged his clenched fist down with a crash onto Townsend's desk. Pens and paper clips sprayed around the room. "Now listen to me, you stuffed up office boy. A lot of far better men than you died down there, including Sanchar. And a lot more would have died if it hadn't been for the RAF and the Navy and a hell of a lot of good luck. You just bloody well sit on your arse in London and take the credit and the gongs. You make me sick, the lot of you."

Townsend could hardly speak. "My God......well, bless my soul." He swallowed hard. "I want an apology now, Richard....at once. If not, I'll....."

"You can stick your job right up your fat bureaucratic backside," Turnbull replied, his face no more than two inches from Townsend's quivering nose. He turned to leave, but as he opened the door, Townsend shouted after him.

"Richard, you don't leave this job....ever. You know that."

"Just watch me," Turnbull answered him and slammed the door closed.

○○

It was a warm, bright early summer's day in London. Despite his heavy suitcase, Turnbull felt invigorated as he left Finchley Road tube station and headed for his flat. He stopped to buy a newspaper at the small newsstand at the bottom of his road. It was good to be back in England, on home ground. The trees outside his apartment block were in full blossom, and although the daffodils had wilted, the tulips were already bursting out in luxurious colour. The lift was broken again, but it didn't seem to matter. After all he'd been through that day, he was dog-tired, but a few gins would do the trick. He was scratching around with the key, when to his astonishment the door opened and Sally stood in front of him, her face streaked with tears. For a moment they just stared at each other. Then Turnbull reached out and took her into his arms.

∞

Nearly two hours later, Turnbull lay quietly, gazing up at the ceiling.

Sally snuggled up close to him.

"It's wonderful to be home with you, darling," she whispered.

He took a deep breath. "I've got some bad news, Sally."

She stiffened.

"I'm afraid I've thrown the job in. You're going to have to keep me for a while."

"But that's marvellous, darling," she replied happily. "You were always too good for that boring old desk job."

Turnbull smiled. "Yes, you're right. I need to look for something a bit more exciting."

Printed in the United Kingdom by
Lightning Source UK Ltd., Milton Keynes
136668UK00001B/29/P